THE BILLIONAIRE
SHIFTER'S
Secret Baby

DIANA SEERE

THE BILLIONAIRE SHIFTER'S SECRET BABY

A masquerade ball in Malibu led to a single night of passion under the stars . . . and set the wheels of fate in motion.

Three years ago, waitress Kara Jablonski gave in to her wilder side with a fellow weretiger, the rock star billionaire Lars Jensen, a sun-kissed blond drummer with a viking's build. Six weeks later, the pregnancy test came back positive.

Knowing Lars' powerful, overbearing mother would be able to take the baby away, Kara did what she had to do.

She hid him.

Now chance has brought Lars back into her life, his touch making her pulse beat like the old legends. So strong, so loud, so bold.

So right.

But can she trust him to want more than another night under the stars? Can she trust him to claim his son as his heir . . . and Kara as his mate?

Fate responds with a roar . . .

The Billionaire Shifter's Secret Baby stars Lars Jensen, a member of a shifter family with viking blood featured in earlier books in the series, and is part of the Howls Romance series as well: *http://howlsromance.com*

One

U nder normal circumstances, Kara Jablonski would've been happy to pause and admire the towering blond god as he strode across the elegant lobby below the Platinum Club. His expensive black suit was obviously custom-made, cut perfectly to his broad shoulders, narrow waist, and powerful thighs. Above the impressive physique, thick hair swept away from his forehead in loose waves, gleaming like gold in the sunlight pouring in through the Boston skyscraper's high windows. His eyes were a piercing cobalt blue. And even more stunning than the rest of him, one perfect dimple indented his chin as if kissed by a naughty, slutty angel.

Right . . . *there*. She could almost feel it under her lips.

Under normal circumstances, she would've taken the time to drink in every inch of him, knowing he'd never notice a girl like her even if she were openly drooling like a starving stray cat.

Meow.

But this was not a normal circumstance.

Heart thudding against her ribs, Kara lifted her bag in front of her face and scurried behind a row of potted ficus trees. After a moment, she risked peeking through the leaves at the god.

No, not a god.

A weretiger.

The breath seeped out of her, leaving her limp. How dare he look so good, so beautiful, so . . . unchanged?

Two years, almost three. But he hadn't aged a day. Of course, shifters had exceptionally long lives, even shifters from the poor, forgotten branches of the breed—like her.

But she was certain she had aged a lifetime in the past two years, almost three. Everything had changed since that night.

Everything.

What was he doing here? If she'd ever thought he would show up in Boston, let alone this building, she never would've taken the waitressing job at the Platinum Club. So far as she knew, he wasn't even an American. He was a globe-trotting playboy, he and his brothers loaded with as much old money as the Stantons, the powerful family of shifters who owned this building.

Well, she assumed they did. When Eva called her about working here, she'd implied as much. Eva, also a shifter of modest means, although not as modest as Kara's, managed the Platinum Club. Eva was always looking for good waitstaff, she'd said, especially lately since there had been unusually high turnover.

He should be out in the world, enjoying his wealth, prestige, and gorgeousness—in both man and tiger form. He shouldn't be parading around Boston when she was just figuring how to get through her life without him, not that she'd ever had her life *with* him, except for that one night. She and Nana had just moved into a two-bedroom apartment, and this job had an elite clientele with a salary to match. A salary they needed desperately.

Where'd he go? She peered through the branches again, an uncontrollable sigh drifting out of her.

He was out of sight and out of her life.

Again.

Another sigh.

Seeing him wasn't only painful, but dangerous. However, as tempted as she was to turn and run out of the building and never look back—perhaps even shifting to speed her escape—she straightened her spine and held her ground.

She couldn't leave. She needed this job. They all did. The days of only thinking of herself had passed.

After waiting another minute, she stepped out from behind the potted trees and walked to the elevator. Although the waitresses had a dressing room they could use before their shifts, Kara preferred to work as she'd arrived, in her favorite black dress and ballet flats. She liked how it made her invisible—or maybe she liked an excuse for why most people didn't notice her, and even men she'd danced with, men she'd kissed, men she'd—Well, even they seemed capable of completely forgetting her. Easier to blame it on her boring clothes than on her face, body, or personality.

He'd walked within five feet of her and hadn't even blinked. Neither one of his golden-lashed eyelids over his sapphire-blue irises had flickered a millimeter. She'd even gasped a little when he'd stepped in front of her. All morning, in fact, she'd been as jumpy as a cat at a pool party, sweating too much, breathing too fast—she'd thought it was nerves about starting the new job.

But it was nerves about him.

The father of her child.

And he didn't even know her name.

⎯⎯⎯

Lars Jensen ate up the ground beneath his feet, the shiny marble of the lobby gleaming. He strode with purpose, here for a meeting with Gavin Stanton and other shifters, convened for a very specific reason: the preservation of the shifter world.

His mind whirling with thoughts of finding the man who seemed hell-bent on destroying their species and way of life, he didn't notice the headache that began in his chest, migrating up his neck to behind one eye, the pulsing a strangely pressured feeling. Not quite pain.

Certainly not pleasure.

It came with a sudden flush, one that curled his fists and tensed all his muscles at once. Thick thighs expanded with muscle as blood roared through him, his cock turned on like a light switch, his heart hammering in his chest.

He'd felt this way once before.

And only once.

She's here, he thought. Eyes narrowing, his gaze darted around the enormous, high-ceilinged lobby, neck turning slowly, searching, scanning, pattern matching like a—

Like a tiger on the hunt for prey.

His nostrils widened, and he smelled her, the intoxicating scent going straight to the root of him, making him drunk and dizzy, vision blurring as he began to breathe heavily.

Control it, he told himself. Pausing before the elevator door, he saw a blur of greenery out of the corner of his eye.

Ding!

Called by technology and disoriented, he climbed into the mouth of the metal beast with a group of humans, all headed upstairs. As the doors closed, the abrupt withdrawal of her scent made it easy to restrain himself, composure returning as quickly as he'd lost it.

"Lars. Good to see you," said a familiar voice, the silky strands of elegant femininity filling the air as he turned to catch the eye of Eva Nagy, the manager of the Platinum Club. She was so much more in the shifter world, but given the abundance of humans surrounding them, he couldn't very well comment on that.

"And you as well, Eva," he said. "Always a joy. How is business?"

"Our members are pleased. That is all that matters," she said smoothly, her voice like warm caramel. Some of the human men in the elevator released a mating scent.

So did some of the women.

"You're here for work?" she asked, making chitchat, knowing damn well why he was here.

"Mmm," he said, noncommittal on purpose. A young woman, barely out of adolescence, made eyes at him, the flirting unmistakable. Under any other circumstance, he would take the bait, though by the looks of her—leggy blonde, overpainted with makeup, tongue rubbing against her lip suggestively—she was more like *jail*bait.

That was not the only reason why he gave her a polite nod and turned away.

"I know you," said the blonde, triggering a running line of memory in Lars. Had he slept with her the last time he'd been in Boston?

"Hello," he said, stalling for time.

"You're Lars Jensen! From The Fates. The drummer." She looked at his hands. "You have some of the finest moves in the music world."

All eyes turned on him. The men were scornful and dismissive. The women released more mating scents.

"Thank you," he said, trying to ease out of the conversation. Her gaze met his, wide and open, clearly interested in what his hands could do for her. "Are you here to play?" Wink.

"I am here on business," he said coldly, anger gratefully replacing whatever feeling he'd encountered in the lobby. He reached into his pocket and pretended to answer a text. The blonde got the message, her face twisting into the nastiness of the rejected. He knew her type.

He despised her type.

The pounding of his heart slowed as each floor dinged, taking them farther away from the lobby. The mystery woman's scent was gone within three deep breaths.

By the time the doors to the Platinum Club opened, he found it easy to convince himself he'd been mistaken. The mysterious woman he'd shared a night of passion with nearly three years ago, who had disappeared without a trace, was not here.

Pulse returning to normal, he walked slowly—achingly slowly—to the room where Gavin and his brother, Derry, were waiting for him.

Foolish hope had reignited in him, whimsy he could ill afford right now.

He had smelled a ghost. The stress of the shifter world's problems had created mixed signals in his mind. She was not here.

His cock, on the other hand, refused to accept the truth.

Two

Within her first hour working tables at the club, Kara already knew she was crazy about Carl, the bartender. Her fellow waitresses were much friendlier than she'd expected, too, for such an exclusive place. They'd taught her the unusual rules of the famously secretive club—no tabs, no tips, just top service and infinite discretion. Although nobody pointed them out, Kara identified quite a few shifters dotted amongst the other members, but they were all strictly in human form, their other natures a secret here, even in a club owned by other shifters.

Most of the members of the Plat were rich and famous humans from politics, sports, and entertainment. There was a senator, that tech billionaire with green hair, and a breakout singer on YouTube who currently was enjoying her first viral pop hit—at seventy-four years old. There was also an actor from HBO whom she'd seen at parties in LA—before she'd found out she was pregnant and left town in a big hurry.

Except for That Night, Kara had never been a guest, of course, only a servant with a tray and a drink, a bottle and an appetizer, smokes and pills. The hard stuff was one reason she'd hated gigs at private homes of the rich and famous. Although she didn't mind serving cocktails, she didn't drink.

Except for That Night, of course.

Eva stepped out from behind the bar, holding her cell phone. "I need your help, Kara. There's a private party. Some relatives of mine"—here she paused and gave Kara a meaningful glance—"have run out of their preferred sustenance. I've been called to provide it. But I'll need you to go down to the wine cellar because I can't leave the floor right now."

"Sure thing," Kara said, thinking it was odd this modern skyscraper had a cellar. It must be a nickname and was actually a modern, climate-controlled room of some kind. "Where is it?"

"You'll need to take the service elevator down. Hit the bottom button. Old thing looks like it'll break any day now, but it's surprisingly resilient." Eva smiled, arching a brow. "Like so many of us." She handed Kara a slip of paper with some French names written on it in an old-fashioned, slanted hand and strode away in her tight navy suit. She seemed to glide rather than walk, like gravity didn't affect her.

Then again, most other people weren't shifters and wouldn't know Eva's cool grace matched her feline form. If she and Kara were related, neither knew which ancestor linked them, although they all had intertwining ties in the Old World if you went back far enough. It was Eva's friendship with Kara's late mother that had inspired her to reach out to her with the job. Although how this elegant professional woman could've been friends with Kara's late mother, who had never held an honest job in her life, was a mystery.

Kara set down her tray on the bar, but just as she began walking to the elevator, she felt something burn down her spine like a river of fire. Inhaling sharply, she staggered forward a step and froze, suddenly aware with every atom of her body that somebody was watching her.

Somebody behind her.

The burning feeling on her back spread down each arm to each fingertip, up to her ears and throat, down to each nipple, then diving between her legs and flooding her with molten need.

Her knees began to tremble. She couldn't look. She couldn't risk it.

You, said a voice. *I've found you.*

Her heart pounded in her ears, but its beat wasn't the only one. She could hear a second pounding in sync with hers, a deafening throb that was louder and deeper than the music from the dance floor next door to the lounge.

You! cried the voice.

It couldn't be. It couldn't. He'd been gentle and strong, he'd given her pleasure she'd never known before or since, they'd laughed and wept and climaxed together, but he would never, ever be able to recognize her. She'd been so careful.

Well, not so careful about the baby thing. But that oversight had turned out to be the greatest joy of her life.

Telling herself it was only nerves and exhaustion—her toddler son had kept her up all night and had skipped his nap that afternoon—Kara snapped herself out of her foolish daze and strode to the hallway with the service elevator.

The trail of heat followed her like a tightrope. She had to fight for each step she took away from him.

No, not him. It couldn't be him. It couldn't.

She stumbled forward into the ancient service elevator and punched the lowest button, leaning her forehead against the cold wall as she tried to catch her breath. Her pulse continued to throb under her skin, making her flushed and restless, aching and hungry. Her nerves tingled with the strain of fighting off an unwanted shift. Her entire life, she'd been afraid of inheriting her mother's bad habit of shifting uncontrollably. It was the kind of thing other shifters looked down on, seeing it as low class.

Kara shook off the sensation, took a deep breath, and looked up.

He stood in the doorway, his blue eyes blazing.

"You," he growled. "It *is* you."

The kiss happened before Lars could stop himself, decency be damned. Decency never made him feel like this. Decency didn't run its tongue along the soft edge of her teeth, her lips pressing against his, her tongue warm, wet, inviting him to explore, to reunite them.

Decency didn't slide its hands up his shoulders, into the thick blond hair at the nape of his neck, moaning in his arms and writhing as he cupped her breast, urgency making him search deeper, the sweet taste of her mouth making him need to taste her everywhere else.

And decency most certainly did not slam her against the elevator wall, sink his hand into her shining chocolate waves, pull her leg up his hip, his cock straining against his trousers to escape as the inadequacy of rubbing against her now-soaked panties had to do.

But decency did force him to stop when the elevator dinged and she froze, all traces of passion draining out of her as she pulled her skirt down and ran her fingers over her face, as if checking to make sure she was still here.

"Wait!" he called out as she practically ran from him, her head turning left and right. She darted into a room, opening a thick, heavy door and disappearing into a dimly lit stone cave-like space before he could catch her.

Dizzy with pure, unadulterated desire, he followed her, eyes adjusting to the dark. Wine bottles gleamed in the low light, half circles shining like voyeurs watching them.

"I don't even know your name!" he said in a low, barely controlled voice, blood pumping desperately through him as if this were the end of the world, his last chance for redemption, his final stand.

A skittering in the corner made him rush to the far back of the room, where he found her leaning against a wood table, hands gripping the edge behind her, facing him. Her chin tipped up with defiance, the stance making her breasts call out to him, nipples like perfect pearls beneath the fabric of her top. Her scent called out to him, seductive and ready. She was a shifter, he knew. A tiger, like him.

The beat of his flashing blood turned stronger until it crowded out all thought, hands clenched to hold back from devouring her, putting his head between her legs and ripping her panties off with his teeth, from giving her what she wanted too.

He smelled it on her.

And as she leaned forward, her eyes in the light, he saw her pupils, two pieces of round onyx, wide for him.

"Kara," she said. "My name is Kara. Please leave me alone."

"Kara." The sounds felt like a puzzle piece that clicked into place in his unfinished heart. "I'm Lars."

Her incredulous laugh felt like mocking. "I know exactly who you are, Lars. Who doesn't know Lars Jensen? Drummer for The Fates, international playboy, wealthy shifter heir." Trying to get past him, she walked in an arc.

He sidestepped and caught her arm.

"Don't leave. You left me that night, nearly three years ago. The party at Woodside. I've spent years trying to find you."

"Why?" He could tell she didn't want to talk.

Too bad.

"Because that night ruined me."

She reeled back as if slapped, two bright red spots on her cheeks. "What?"

"Ruined me for other women."

"Your reputation precedes you. If I ruined you for other women, you have a funny way of showing it, Mr. Playboy."

"Do you always believe rumors? Stereotypes are for the weak."

Her nostrils flared, the reaction surprising as she clenched her jaw and gave him a look of unfiltered rage. She ripped her arm out of his and looked at a piece of paper. "I need to do my job. Some of us have to work for a living. Am I being stereotypical?" Her smirk cut him like a blade to the heart.

He snatched the paper out of her hand and quickly found the three bottles listed, holding them hostage. "Have I offended you?" Confusion made his head spin more, the beat in his lungs, his heart, every organ he possessed making it hard to think.

Without a word, she reached for the wine bottles. He pulled them away.

"I've clearly upset you. Let me make it up to you with dinner. Your favorite restaurant. Tonight."

"No." She started toward the doorway.

Determination made his blood beat faster. "Please," he said, drawing the word out, turning it into a caress. She halted right before the door, turned around, and marched back to him. He set the bottles down on a large butcher-block table, the top scarred and rubbed to a fine patina, old and well used.

Her eyes flitted to the bottles, then back to his face. The evolution of her emotions captivated him, her scent overwhelming. She evoked so much. He couldn't help himself, stepping forward, fingertips on her tight jaw, lips lightly brushing hers as he punctuated the *please* with so much more. The word needed an action, a caress.

A kiss.

This time Kara was the one who took it further, surprising Lars, making him bloom with unbridled, craven need. Her hands played at his waist, unbuckling his pants, the zipper's release a love song. She stroked him, his hand hungrily eating her skin, riding up to squeeze her ass as she—

Click click click.

The doorway. Someone was entering.

Cool air struck him suddenly as Kara shoved him away so hard he knocked into the table. One of the bottles wobbled and started to fall, feet away from shattering on the stone floor.

Kara dived and caught it with the reflexes of a cat.

And that was how Eva found them, disheveled and breathing hard, Kara bent at his feet in supplication, holding a wine bottle at his knees, his legs wide, belt unbuckled, pants open.

Eva sighed, her eyes rolling to the right, an uncharacteristic display of emotion from the ice queen. She looked around the wine cellar, muttering something to herself. Then she caught Lars' eye and said:

"Who put a magic spell on this wine cellar? What is it with you shifter men?"

Without another word, she exited.

Three

K ara knew she had to get away from him. She jumped to her feet, flushed with lust, shame, and fury. "I told you to leave me alone!" she cried, cradling the bottles of wine at her chest as she hurried out of the room. The floor was cobblestone, far older than the building above them. It truly was a cellar, probably hundreds of years old.

"Kara," he called after her, his voice like a song. The sound of her name on his lips made her pause, longing for him. But then she pictured little Jamie's face, so similar to his father's, and found the willpower to keep moving.

If Lars ever saw Jamie, he would know. Those eyes, such a particular blue, the white-gold hair, and that dimple. Given his fame, even strangers would joke about how much the two-year-old baby looked like the famous blond drummer. Of course they were joking, assuming there was no way a curvy, unglamorous waitress could have had the rock god's baby.

But Lars would know. If he ever saw Jamie, he would know instantly.

And he couldn't ever, ever know. His family would take Jamie from her and kick her out in the cold. They had the wealth and power to separate mother and baby forever, out of the reach of any law or country. Whatever sexual attraction was sparking between Lars and her now—and a few years ago—was only chemistry. The mystery of her name, her hidden face, her disappearance—this alone had fed his interest. It wasn't serious, and it wouldn't last.

But her love for her baby was serious and forever. She couldn't let the wealthy Jensens rip her little family apart, and they would. A baby weretiger with Lars' dimples? Those sparkling pure-blue eyes and chubby pink cheeks? His Jensen relatives would claim him and fight to own him—with teeth and claw.

She couldn't let them ever find out about Jamie. Whatever she had to do, whatever she had to sacrifice, she would.

"Kara," he said softly behind her. He didn't grab her, but he was close enough to smell.

Although given the heightened senses of her lust at the moment, she could've smelled him in Denmark.

She stabbed the elevator button, cursing the lack of a modern stairwell. This place was dangerous.

"Dinner tomorrow," he said. "I'll be a gentleman. We'll talk, learn about each other. Tell me where to send the car and—"

"We can't—" she began to say, but stopped herself. If she refused him now, he'd follow her, demand she change her mind, make a scene at the bar, maybe even follow her home.

To Jamie. She couldn't risk that.

The elevator arrived, and she stepped in. Without looking up at him, she hit the button for the Platinum Club. "We can't be seen together here again. Give me a number where I can reach you."

He placed one strong leg in front of the elevator door, blocking it open, and pulled out his phone. "Tell me yours, and I'll send you mine."

Again, she couldn't risk it. Pushing his knee away from the

door, she rattled off a number with a Boston area code and hoped he wouldn't discover it was fake until she was safely out of the building and on the bus home.

The door closed, leaving her alone inside the car with the three bottles of wine, and as it rose up to the Platinum Club, she wondered what she was going to tell Eva. Quitting in the middle of her first shift would need a good excuse. Cancer? Aliens?

When Carl saw her reappear on the floor, he stepped out from behind the bar and took the bottles out of her arms. "Eva wants to talk to you. Her office."

Kara let out a breath. Looks like she wasn't going to have to quit; Eva was going to fire her. "Thanks."

He gave her a sympathetic look. "Nice knowing you."

Instead of laughing, she felt a wave of sadness. This would've been a nice place to work. "You too." Before he'd see her start to cry, she spun away and strode to Eva's office.

Eva stood at the window, looking out on Boston from a dozen floors up. "Don't tell me," she said. "You think you're going to leave us."

Kara paused in the middle of Eva's tastefully elegant office. "I figured you were firing me."

"Of course not. It's not your fault shifter men seem to be drawn to that wine cellar like bees to honey."

Throat dry, Kara struggled to find words. "There's something else. Some other reason I can't stay."

"The baby," Eva said.

Kara gasped. She'd been so careful. Nobody in Boston knew, and Kara had made few friends back in LA, none of whom ever found out she'd gotten pregnant. Nana never spoke to strangers, and Kara had given a friend's address on her tax paperwork.

"How . . ."

"Sometimes I know things," Eva said. "Let's just leave it at that."

"You spied on me." Kara looked around Eva's office, wondering what else the cool, clever woman knew. "Was that why you offered me the job?"

"You're a skilled waitress," Eva said, "and my club needed one."

"You didn't know my mother, did you?" Panic rose in Kara's gut. "Did Lars send you? Is he looking for me? Does he—"

"Calm yourself. Lars knows nothing. And I did know your mother, although we were only acquaintances. She was traveling in Europe with a very handsome green-eyed werewolf who adored her but was prone to getting in fights. The jealous type, I believe."

Kara crossed her arms over her chest. "My father," she said in a low voice. "I never knew him. He died when I was a baby." In a fight to the death with the bear shifter who became her stepfather. Briefly. He left when she was seven, and Kara barely remembered him. The first of many stepfathers.

"I can appreciate why you want to build a happy family of your own," Eva said.

"If the Jensens find out about Jamie—"

"Jamie," Eva said. "A boy?"

"James," Kara said softly. "He's my life."

"He's part of your life. There could be more."

Kara looked out at the city lights, sending her thoughts out to her little one, her bright heart. "I can't risk losing him for anything." She took a deep breath. "I'm sorry, but I can't work here after all. I didn't realize how many shifters would be here at the Platinum Club. I expected the Stantons, but—"

"Lars is only here for a meeting with the Stantons over a

security matter. Nobody expects him to stay or to return." Eva walked over to her desk and tapped a screen. "His personal jet is scheduled to fly to Tokyo the day after tomorrow. His rooms at the Mandarin are booked through the rest of the month."

"He thinks we're having dinner together," she said softly.

"When?"

Her mind was spinning. "Tomorrow, I suppose. I gave him a fake number."

"Then I expect to be hearing from him very shortly."

"That's why I have to leave," Kara said.

"Why run? He'll find you. He's a predator, Kara. When you bolted, his instincts were to chase you down. Perhaps, if you want to get rid of him, you should stand firm, at least for one meal."

Hadn't Kara suspected the same thing, that he was only interested in her because she'd run away? "But if he sees . . . If he finds out about . . ."

"Leave the infant with his nanny. I suspect that the dining establishments Lars frequents are not the kind to have booster chairs and chicken nuggets."

The thought of seeing him again—not for sex but talking and laughing with one another like friends—filled her with warmth. She'd missed him. They'd only had one evening together, but she'd felt a bond between them. It hadn't lasted, but she'd felt that, under different circumstances, in a different life, they could've been close.

"You're sure he's leaving the country?" Kara asked.

"After Japan, he's due to move into his new home in Tuscany. He only comes to the States for brief visits." Eva gave her a pointed look. "His mother died last year, and his father lives overseas."

One dinner. How dangerous could it be? "If he comes to

you, could you tell him to pick me up here at seven? I'm on the lunch shift."

Smiling coolly, Eva ushered her to the door. "Certainly. And may I remind you that right now you are on the evening shift? Carl is probably pulling his hair out, and at his age he'll cry over each strand lost."

———

By the time he reached the Novo Club and the elevator doors opened, he knew the number she'd given him was fake. Halfway through dialing it, he stopped, closed his eyes, and focused.

Oh what those few kisses had done to him. No stranger to women who offered their bodies like beads in a Mardi Gras parade, Lars had tasted plenty of women over the years. His body responded, enjoying the wilder, forbidden lust of two bodies joining for the pure sake of pleasure. No walls, no boundaries, no self-consciousness, no judgment.

Just touch and taste and slick and musk, all rolled together in bedsheets, bent over countertops and tables, pressed against high-rise patio doors and garden courtyard brick walls. Being in a rock band meant groupies. Human women, shifter women—he wasn't particular.

Just *women* would do.

Shifters knew who he was, though. As a Jensen, he held power and wealth that many ambitious women found appealing. Sniffing out a fake from the real thing was an art form.

But nothing gave him what she gave. No woman made him feel such depth. Such authenticity. No woman made him crave like Kara.

"Kara," he whispered to himself. *Kara.* Now she had a name.

A location. Eva knew her. Kara worked at the Plat. Nearly three years of questions all answered in one chance encounter.

One kiss.

Okay, more than one kiss . . .

"Lars!" boomed a deep voice, unmistakable in its tone. Only Derry Stanton could make stone vibrate with his deep bear-shifter voice. A reformed cad and one of Lars' favorite party-scene friends, the ex-playboy was recently engaged to be married.

Pigs should be flying. Pig shifters, of course.

The two shook hands, Lars holding his own, as the secret club's butler appeared out of a dark nook. Morgan was older than the Dead Sea scrolls, and Lars found the man infuriatingly dull. But he was a stalwart figure in the exclusive, secret shifter club, buried deep in the bowels of the Boston, Massachusetts subway system, and Lars gave him a polite greeting.

"The usual, Mr. Jensen?" Morgan asked, knowing Lars' penchant for dark lager beer.

A simple nod and the man disappeared, leaving Derry to plant one of those baseball glove-sized hands on Lars' shoulder and ask quietly, "Who is she?"

"That obvious?"

"You smell like pussy."

"I am a cat."

"That joke never gets old for you felines, does it? My brother flogs it too."

Lars laughed, appreciating the diversion. The Stanton family, unlike the Jensens, was a motley crew, a mix of wolf, bear, and lion shifters. The Jensens were all tigers. Shifter DNA was a complex mystery, more magic than science, and the quest for research was ongoing.

And was the very reason Lars was in Boston.

He tensed at the thought. "Any word on Tomas Nagy's location?" Recently one of their own had turned against them, stealing blood and serum samples that unlocked shifter DNA secrets. Tomas Nagy had created a biological weapon that could destroy shifter culture—and possibly kill all shifters, if unchecked.

Time was of the essence in finding Tomas, controlling the weapon, and bringing peace to the shifter world once more.

Until he had run into Kara—how odd to think of her by name!—Lars had been consumed by the hunt for Tomas Nagy.

Now he had solved a completely different missing persons case.

"Drink first. Settle down," Derry said softly, leading Lars to a comfortable wingback chair by a roaring fire. Soft, cracked leather met his tense hands as he settled in, a thin layer of foam kissing the top of the pint of beer Morgan set on the table next to him. Dim lighting from dark sconces on the stone walls made the room both warm and cold at the same time. Tipping his head up to drink, Lars let his gaze soar to the top of the arched ceilings, the sense of boundless space unsettling, given their subterranean quarters.

"So?" he prodded.

"Asher says Tomas' exact position has been pinpointed. For now. He's nowhere near the United States, but we don't know more than that." Asher was Derry's eldest brother, the patriarch of the Stanton clan and arguably one of the leaders, if not *the* leader, of the shifter world. "Gavin says that his biotech firm is feverishly studying shifter DNA to halt any biological weapons Tomas creates."

Lars wanted to relax. The news was positive but not encouraging. He sighed.

"Never forget," his father had once told him. "Shifters created the Novo Club to hide from those who seek to kill us. Eradicate us. Make us disappear."

No one suspected that one of their own might be the source of that destruction.

He guzzled half the beer, desperate to shake the strange melancholy that hit him suddenly. Derry gave him a puzzled half grin, a long, slow inhale making it clear Lars was being studied.

"Pussy," Derry replied, his face splitting with a lascivious grin. "But only one scent."

"It's a long story."

"I've got nothing better to do. Gavin is running a few minutes late." With long, dark brown hair, so inky it was nearly black, and incongruously blue eyes that had always put Lars at ease, Derry was an unlikely confidante.

Eh. What the hell.

"Fine," Lars said with a sigh. "I met a woman."

"Clearly."

"Nearly three years ago. We were at a costume party."

"Let me guess. You went as a tiger."

"That joke is never funny."

"Neither is the cat joke."

"Do you want to hear my story?"

"Any story involving sex is one I want to hear."

Lars took a long drink, then continued. "It was one of those charity balls. You know the kind. We attend because our families write enormous checks to keep the human world happy and off our trails. And because the charities do good. My father needed one of us to go, and so I went. Got my band to play. Why not, right? Might as well up the 'good patron' image and have some fun while I was at it."

Derry blinked rapidly, nodding slowly. Lars could speak in shorthand with the Stanton men. They got it. Being from one of the old, wealthy shifter families wasn't quite as bad as being British royalty, but close. A life lived under the microscope wasn't all it was cracked up to be.

Sometimes you had to make it fun. Take your enjoyment where you could.

And shifters walked a fine line. Pretend in the human world while meeting shifter needs.

"So I went as the Beast from *Beauty and the Beast*," Lars explained.

"Oh, how original," Derry intoned, his snort punctuating his amusement.

Lars shrugged. "I'm built for it." Derry's arched eyebrow made him laugh. "Not like *you*, but I'm certainly no church mouse." All of the Jensen men were tall, Viking blood running through them. Lars was Derry's height but leaner.

"Let me guess," Derry said drolly. "She was Belle."

"Clichéd. I know. I played a set with the band. Went for a drink. Saw her. Walked up to her, prepared to have her in a coatroom beneath me, skirts up and deep in her between sets, but that's not what happened. At all."

The warm comfort of sweet memory glowed within him. No, it wasn't just the beer. Even mental images didn't do their night together justice. No words he could blurt out to Derry Stanton could convey how Kara had made him *feel*.

"You fell for her."

"I did." Lars expected judgment, and before Derry had met his fiancée, Jess, he would have been roundly taunted for letting one woman bring him to his knees.

All he heard in Derry's voice was profound understanding.

Morgan appeared with a new beer as Lars finished his last swallow. The cold foam of the fresh pint broke through the haze of memory, so tangible, so palpable he could almost feel Kara's heartbeat in every inch of his skin.

Impossible.

"And?"

"And I never learned her name. Silly, I know. She wore a small mask. Had a different hairstyle. The ball was held at a grand oceanside hotel where I had a beach bungalow at the resort. We made love under a blanket of stars. When I woke up in the morning, she was gone."

"Did she leave a glass slipper? Escape in a pumpkin?"

"No," Lars said seriously, too caught up in his own twisted emotions to take the bait. "I wish. She left me with nothing. Nothing but a ragged hole in my chest where my heart was supposed to be."

"She's the scent on you? Right now?" Derry inhaled again. "It's a woman I do not know."

Lars felt jealousy rush through his veins as if his blood had turned green. "Good."

"I didn't mean—my good man—I . . ." Derry shut up quickly. Even he couldn't defend his old manwhore ways.

"She's here," Lars confessed. "I ran into her in the elevator. She works at the Plat now. I met her in California and chased her for months, with no trace of her anywhere. And now I'm here in Boston because of this crazy Tomas mess and *bam!*—here she is."

"Careful of those Plat waitresses," Derry said, not bothering to hide his mischievous grin. "One minute you're sleeping with three women in a limo, and the next minute you're kissing one

THE BILLIONAIRE SHIFTER'S *Secret Baby*   25

under the mistletoe and bam! Gatorade all over your face and you're feeling The Beat."

Lars looked pointedly at Derry's scotch in his hand. "What was that string of words supposed to mean? Have you had too much to drink?"

"Never mind. It means that if she's your One, your fated mate, you'll know."

I think I already do.

Four

Kara finished her first evening and then worked a few hours over the lunch shift the next day, every moment expecting to see Lars appear over her shoulder, at her table, in the elevator where he pulled her into his arms, slid a hand behind her neck, and drew her up to his mouth for a long, sweet kiss.

She didn't see him. But apparently, he did contact Eva, who had told Kara that he would be sending the car to her house later that evening.

"Not my house." Kara had gasped. "He can't know where I live." If he saw Jamie . . .

"It's hopeless. He'll sniff you out one way or another. This way he feels in control and not suspicious. If you insist on meeting him here, he'll know you have something to hide." Eva had patted her on the shoulder. "I told him you'd meet him downstairs."

And so Kara had finished her shift and gone home before dinner, only half-aware of her surroundings, caught up in memories of That Night.

When he'd been in costume as the Beast, she'd been powerfully drawn to him, almost against her will. Surrounded by wealthy socialites, media stars, and celebrities, she'd been afraid of him, but because she was masked, wearing a beautiful gown a friend had lent her, and loaded with liquid courage, she was able to reply when he'd walked up to her.

"Release my father," she'd declared, pretending to be Belle.

He'd paused only a second, glaring at her down his bulbous fake nose before hooking an enormous hand around her waist and drawing her to the dance floor.

Magic. Hearts beating as one, drowning in each other's eyes, all of it. The other guests gave them room and clapped, seeing the chemistry, the moment in time, the fairy tale. And then Beauty and Beast danced another song, and another, until he led her to the edge of the floor and then out a pair of doors to a stone balcony overlooking the garden. Again, like a fairy tale, except this one was in Malibu. The garden gave way to a cliff and then sand and the salty, wild waves of the Pacific.

"Tell me your name," he'd said.

"Tell me yours," she'd teased. Because at that moment she still hadn't figured out who he was, not having arrived in time to see him play with the band, although she knew, of course, that he was a shifter. How wonderful to meet one of her own kind here among the Hollywood royalty. She hoped he was like her, an interloper, a party crasher, an exile.

"I asked you first," he'd said.

"You didn't ask," she'd replied. "You demanded."

He'd pressed her against the stone railing, his hips hard against hers, his desire obvious. "I'm about to demand a lot more," he said, growling in her ear. "You know that, don't you?"

"You're taking your time about it."

Now, remembering, Kara felt embarrassed at herself. She'd been playing a game. She'd been caught up in a dream. Never before or since had she acted like that.

"If you don't want me to take you," he'd said, his voice strained, "you'd better tell me now. And then leave me. I'm not myself. I want . . . I want you more than anyone, more than anything, and I don't even know who you are."

"I'm not going anywhere." She'd slid her hands up his neck and tunneled them through his hair, the thick blond locks visible behind the mask.

"You're a tiger," he'd whispered, dragging his teeth across the pulse in her throat. "I can smell you." And then he'd inhaled her scent like an inverse roar, lifted her into his arms, and carried her down the steps to the beach below.

There had been a bungalow. It had been after sunset, cold outside from the evening chill but warm inside, sheltered in his arms.

When he'd taken off the mask and she'd realized whose beautiful, large, muscled, naked body she was straddling, it had been too late to run away.

As if she ever would have said no to him.

But could she now?

Kara got off the bus in a daze, suddenly reminded of the present day. Boston. Years later. Her baby at home, waiting for her.

Their baby.

She would say no to him now because she had a reason to. Because she had to.

Another few blocks and she was entering the apartment she was determined to make a home. "Hi, it's me!" she called out, hearing the TV playing and Jamie's shouting and laughing from the other room. There were only two rooms other than the kitchen, but it was enough for now. Nana had the bedroom, she and Jamie had the living room. Most people in the world did with far less—just as she had for most of her life. She did wish she could give Jamie his own room, though, with murals of lizards and trucks and spaceships on the walls, and kid-sized furniture embroidered with his initials, a bed shaped like a race car, and . . .

There was a lot she wanted to give him.

"Welcome back, Mommy," Nana said. That was what Nana always called Kara, although she was at least sixty years older, maybe more. She also insisted that Kara (and everyone else) call her Nana instead of her real name, which she refused to admit was Bertha Lucretia Nowakowski. (Kara saw it on her bank statement.) An impoverished shifter like Kara, Nana had been making her living as a servant for her entire life, usually caring for children but also working as housekeeper, cook, and elder companion to wealthier shifters. Her last employer had fired her when she'd been too old to work as hard as he'd wanted. Even by shifter standards, Nana was ancient, many decades older than she appeared. Now she and Kara looked out for each other. "We've had a nice day, haven't we, Jamie baby?"

"Mama!" Jamie ran—with the long, loping grace of a cat—into Kara's arms. "Appo joose!"

"No juice, sorry kiddo." It was bad for his teeth, the pediatrician at the clinic had warned, and a tiger shifter would need every one.

In protest, he wriggled out of her arms and jumped onto the sofa.

"I'm going out again tonight," Kara told them both. "Dinner with a friend."

Nana gave her a narrow-eyed stare. She was a sharp old lady. "Be careful."

"I will," Kara said firmly. "Very."

"Then we'll see you before midnight," Nana said.

Kara paused only a moment. "Of course you will."

"Humph." Nana reclined on the sofa next to Jamie and gestured at the kitchen. "He had macaroni and cheese for a late snack and skipped his afternoon nap, so I think he'll go down early."

"I'll give him a bath. Would you like to get clean, little guy?" Kara cooed.

Nana laughed. "Lucky he's a tiger like you, loves the water. I can't tell you how impossible it is to get a lion shifter toddler into the bath. Needs a father to hold him down and spray him with a hose."

Nana herself was a bear shifter and loved the water. She was also blessed with the height and girth of the breed and was probably able to wrestle any child into water by herself, even a lion with all his permanent teeth.

"Bath! Whoo-hoo!" Jamie punched the air with his fists and tore off his clothes. "Nakie tie! Nakie tie!" That was toddler for *naked time*. The boy could *not* keep his clothes on.

"Just like his father," Kara muttered.

Nana perked up. "Is that so? Now what makes you mention him all of a sudden?"

"No reason at all." Kara picked up her naked toddler and brought him to their tiny bathroom for his favorite thing in the whole world.

Other than his mommy, of course.

She gave him extra bubble bath and every one of his water toys, giving him more attention than usual, swimming in love as he swam in the shallow water.

My baby, she thought. *I can't let them ever take my baby.*

Lars stared in dawning horror at his smartphone map app.

"She lives . . . there?" He barely knew Boston, but even he had heard about the small, crime-ridden neighborhood where the GPS told him Kara lived. Headlines nationwide screamed about a string of women kidnapped and held as breeding factories for some sort of survivalist cult.

Dear God. That wasn't why she'd disappeared nearly three years ago, was it?

He snorted, the sound less about humor and more about his own disturbed mind. Of course not. But knowing she lived in a neighborhood so close to such evil filled him with a rush of protective adrenaline.

He had to see her. *Now.*

"This can't be." He looked at the chauffeur, one Eva had called for him, a no-name who seemed wet behind the ears and eager to please. "I'll need you to take me."

"No, sir, please," protested the man, a young human male with a wisp of beard and panicked brown eyes. "I can do the job. I'll go directly to her door and walk her out to the limo myself." He patted a gun holster beneath his jacket.

Lars silenced him with a glare. By the time they were out of the parking garage and headed toward her apartment, he was in the back seat, already busy reading emails, scrolling to find the important one.

His inbox was a file full of fail.

Band bookings. A trust fund form that required a signature. Pictures of naked body parts sent from fans who managed to find his private email address. A message from his father, Ragnar, informing him of a Swedish royalty event seven months from now that Lars would be expected to attend.

More creative fan nudity. One woman had taken a picture of him and Photoshopped her nude body so that she rode him while he played. Clever, but one slip of a drumstick . . .

"Aha!" he gasped with pleasure, the grin involuntary as he read the message from his assistant marked "CONFIDENTIAL."

Sir, this report is incomplete. It's taken from public record in California. Our private records search will be completed shortly. However, per your request, we are sending the information as it comes in.

He downloaded the PDF and read, eyes narrowing as he took in the dossier on Kara Jablonski.

Twenty-four. Tiger shifter. Came from a family whose name he did not recognize. Born in Arizona but raised in California. She'd finished high school and taken some community college. A handful of color photos showed her in dance garb, teaching small children in a light-filled studio with honey-colored floors and large windows.

Her smile was radiant.

A list of all her former addresses, a crime report showing two speeding tickets from six years ago. A mention that the California treasury held $19.11 in unclaimed money for overpayment on a cable bill from a few years ago.

That was it. Even internet searches brought up very little about her. Who lived a life so . . . obscure? So out of the spotlight? In a world where social media drove everyone to create a "personal brand" and turn pictures of dinner into travelogues, her sparse online history was refreshing.

And it abruptly ended nearly three years ago.

Right around That Night.

She'd lived in the LA area, in a corner of Pasadena that certainly wasn't along the Rose Bowl parade route. So little information was available on her. Both parents dead. Both parents shifters. Until a few months ago, he'd have assumed both parents were shifters—of course—because centuries of shifter history had told their world that only two shifters could reproduce and create a shifter.

He tensed as the driver took a hard left, his throat thick with anger. Tomas Nagy—one of their own in the shifter world—had taken valuable shifter genetics research and turned it into a weapon against the rest of their kind.

And Kara was part of their world too.

The limousine stopped in front of a three-story building with porches on the front of each floor. The decking sagged, each floor worse than the next. Checking the surroundings, he emerged from the car only to find Kara rushing out the front door, breathless and before him in seconds, racing to him.

Oh, what a visual feast. Swapping flats for high heels, Kara's long legs looked like they went on forever as she ran to him, calves taut and stretched, a glimpse of sweet, silky thigh making his blood pump harder. She was sophisticated and awkward, defiant and willing, a paradox of wonder all wrapped up in a succulent, sexy package.

Fate worked in mysterious ways.

"Hi," she rasped, pulling a thin gray shawl about her shoulders, a creamy expanse of toned skin making his mouth go dry. Still in the same black dress she'd worn at the Plat, she'd changed her shoes to high heels and added simple silver jewelry. Red lipstick, a bit of thick black eyeliner, and a sweet, spicy scent that made him want to bury his face in her forever.

"Hello. You didn't have to rush. I was going to meet you at your—"

Wheels screeched on pavement a few streets away, the sound of metal and screams muffled in the distance.

"Let's go," he said tersely, ushering her into the car, giving her apartment building one last, unsettling look as he pressed the palm of his hand against her soft back, right where the shawl's edge met the dress's zipper. She was so warm, the smooth fabric drawing him in.

As he climbed in beside her and slid across the supple tan leather seats, he thought: tonight is her last night living in this hovel. I'll see to it.

He'd move her out of here in mere hours.

As they drove away, her scent filled the small space, making him lose all capacity for thought. His fingers twitched against his thighs, desperate to touch her, but she was skittish. Her top teeth sank into the flesh of her full lower lip, smearing her lipstick, as she nervously bit down.

She gave him a shy smile, cheeks plumping like apples. The front of her dress dropped low, showing off cleavage, a small café au lait birthmark right on the edge of the valley between her supple breasts.

Just as he remembered. It had branded his dreams for two years.

Ah, God. This was torture.

"Thanks for picking me up."

He couldn't help it.

Tigers are made for lunging. No sane person could blame him.

Lars was, after all, just giving in to instinct.

Five

Knocked off balance, Kara didn't have the coordination to push him away. Lars seemed to be here, there, everywhere, his clever hands catching her shoulder, her hip, sliding down one thigh over the skirt of her dress and then up the bare skin of the other. When she gasped, his mouth closed over hers, swallowing her fear, her protests, her consciousness.

Oh, he felt so good, he felt so right. The sharp graze of a fingernail behind her ear aroused her, reminding her of his animal side, the same as hers and so, so much more like her than the alienating all-human men she'd settled for in the past. She and he shared something that a Josh or Jake or Ethan never could. They were shifters, unlike the majority cultures of the world who could live loud and open, oblivious to the strange creatures walking amongst them.

Lars was strange like her, a waitress who could smell the lingering hint of oregano in the omelette the driver had had for breakfast or the perfume his girlfriend had worn when he'd made love to her the night before. What normal woman would be able to hear the laughter of the man in the passing bus and even smell the sexual interest of the woman sitting in the seat behind him—as well as what *she* had eaten for lunch? Even after the limo turned and began cruising in the opposite direction?

No normal man would be happy with such a mate for long, certainly not forever. And she was a forever kind of girl, even more now that she was a mother.

"Kara," he moaned against her cheek, then licked the seam of her lips, demanding she open to him.

Hot, steamy need flooded her body. It had been so damn long since she'd touched a man. This man, as it happened. The ridiculousness of it, and her nerves, made her giggle.

"Yes, darling," Lars whispered, "enjoy yourself, and I'll enjoy *you*."

The hand that had slid up her leg was now pushing between the fullness of her thighs to the juncture above, where she ached for him. If those clever fingers reached her panties, he'd know how much.

"Wait," she said, her voice hoarse. She wiggled on the seat, twisting away from the strong, warm hand between her thighs. "You said you were taking me to dinner."

"The restaurant is not, as it happens, in this neighborhood," he growled, following her and replacing his hand. He flicked a tongue over her earlobe. "We have time to reacquaint ourselves a little."

She wrapped her fingers around his wrist to stop its ascent up her legs. As a shifter, her strength was at least twice that of most women, even in human form, but her power was no match for his. His hand settled over her damp panties and pressed into her mound. Sucking in a breath, she leaned against him for a moment, so tempted to let her knees fall open and recline onto her back right there in the limo. The window between the back seat and the driver was closed, smoky black, opaque. She would've bet her tiny savings account that the barrier was soundproof as well.

It would be so good.

So bad. Deliciously bad.

No. She couldn't do this. She wouldn't bring another life into the world without a father or the peace and security of a financially independent mother. Lars would be happy to knock her up again—oh God, that sent tingles up and down her spine and poured more electric heat between her legs—but she couldn't afford another baby. How could she bring another child into poverty? Not now. Not yet. And not with . . .

"Lars," she said firmly. "Is this all you want from me?"

She knew it was, of course it had to be, but asking him the question would force him to behave like a gentleman—at least for a few minutes, during which she could regain her composure. Perhaps by then they'd be at the restaurant.

If there really *was* a restaurant. What if this whole thing was a ruse to fuck her brains out in the limo?

Mmm, that got her hot again.

Damn it!

She'd expected him to grin at her question and kiss her again, assuring her sweetly that of course he wanted more, much more, and she wouldn't believe him because he would hook his fingers under her panties and stroke her to confuse her while whispering his sweet, tempting lies.

But to her shock, he removed his hand and withdrew, putting more than a few inches between them on the leather seat. And he actually looked chagrined. Head down, he balled his hands into fists in his lap and said, "Forgive me, Kara. I don't know what's come over me."

And his tone was sincere.

She laughed nervously. "Me either." And then added, "I mean

me. I'm really not like this. You must have the totally wrong idea about me."

His head turned, and he locked his stunning blue gaze on hers. "I don't think so," he said softly. "If fact, I think I have the perfectly right idea about you."

Although that idea was probably how she was a slut who frequently had quickies with strange men, she found herself feeling that he meant something deep, soulful, romantic.

Just as a shiver swept over every inch of her skin, the limo came to a halt, and a voice came over the speaker. "We're here, Mr. Jensen."

Lars didn't break his gaze. "Sixty seconds," he said.

"Yes, sir," the voice replied.

Why did this man have so much power over her? She felt a stabbing ache in her chest, on her left breast, and wondered if she was having a heart attack. At that moment, nothing on earth could've made her look away from him.

She needed to break the spell somehow. She couldn't let herself pretend this was more than a dream.

She needed him to stop looking at her like a very large, hungry cat with a bowl of cream.

Like a lifeline, her conversation with Eva replayed in her mind. Something about his mother . . .

"I was sorry to hear about your mother's passing," she blurted.

As she'd hoped, a shadow came over his eyes, giving her a much-needed release from the powerful gaze. "Yes," he said and then inhaled deeply. "My father has had a difficult year. They were very happy together."

"I know," she said.

His eyebrows arched. "You did?"

"The Jensen family is famous, even to nobodies like me." She smiled to show she accepted her lowly position in the shifter diaspora with good humor. Although the Stantons were the most powerful shifters in North America, the Jensens were famous—not just Lars and his rock band but his mother, too. Hilda Jensen had been a rich, powerful woman in fashion who had dominated the style pages in New York and in LA. Her control over her handsome sons was also famous. Any woman who got involved with her precious boys was ruthlessly screened, threatened, or bought off. And everyone knew she was always on the lookout for a suitable wife for each of them—so she could be a grandmother. A very fashionable one.

Hilda Jensen's reputation was why Kara had been so quick to flee. A woman like that would never accept Kara and would have all the means to take Jamie.

Except now she was dead.

The thought struck her like a bullet, shutting down further thought.

And then the door opened, and the driver reached inside for her hand.

———

Lars had chosen the restaurant for dinner based on one singular goal: privacy. While the quality of the food was important, the quality of the company tonight was far superior. He needed to keep her away from the prying eyes of other men, away from crowds or overbearing fans seeking a photo op with him, away from any distraction that might make her second-guess their relationship.

Relationship.

When she'd expressed her condolences about his mother, he'd reeled, the unexpected empathy making the world tilt slightly. That simple, polite gesture was everything, triggering an unpredictable anger in him.

She'd known who he was. She knew who his mother was.

She'd known and never sought him out.

Why? He had to know.

The desire for other women faded like the blush on her cheeks as they settled in at a secluded booth in the old downtown steak house, known for two centuries of serving food to Boston blue bloods. While his blood was decidedly more shifter than blue, a table had been made ready instantly when his assistant had called.

"This place is amazing," Kara murmured, taking in the arts-and-crafts feel, the stone walls, the uneven flooring as she moved toward the middle of the booth.

He sat next to her, surprise evident in her features as she moved that round, firm ass further toward the wall.

"You're amazing, Kara."

"Aren't you, um, going to sit across from me?"

He answered with his palm, turning it from the top of her thigh, moving toward the sweet warmth that pulled him in like a magnet.

"I'll take that as a no." She gasped, clearing her throat to mask the desire he heard, her voice going high and light as if his touch made her float.

A gentleman, he knew, would never be so obvious.

But Lars Jensen wasn't known for being a gentleman.

A faceless waiter delivered wine and took their orders, flawless service that made him seem invisible. Good. Lars wanted Kara to see only him. To feel only him. And for him to exist only for her.

Fingertips achingly close to her sweet clit, he paused, not wanting to scare her off. Chin tipped down, she looked up at him with a coquettish, flirty manner. "Is this," she asked, her hand closing over his under her dress, "how you start all your first dates?"

He wanted to smile but settled for locking eyes with her, emotion overpowering him.

"No, Kara. This is how I start my last date."

"You . . . you don't want to see me again?"

"I don't want to date anyone but you. Ever. And I don't want to just *date* you."

"Don't hold back, Lars," she said with a nervous laugh, eyes widening, clearly unnerved. "Tell me how you really feel."

"Don't joke. I'm not. I'm telling you the truth, Kara. All of the truth. We've wasted nearly three years apart. I won't settle for a single second more."

"You come on strong." Those beautiful hazel eyes watched him, wary yet challenging, an intoxicating blend of shyness and confidence that mesmerized him.

Kara reached for her wineglass, twirled the stem, and as if second-guessing herself, took a large gulp, the long, elegant line of her neck begging for his mouth.

As he watched her, she formed an aura, a strange glow no other woman had ever possessed. It throbbed, much like his cock now, and a dawning hunger took over as he realized her glow and his need were in sync.

"There's no other way for me to be when I'm with you," he said. The words came out low and needy, like a warning growl. His hand touched hers, a spark fusing them, the beat clear and all consuming.

"Now you're just using pickup lines." Her words teased him,

but he saw the thin vein at the base of her throat begin to gallop, pounding against her translucent skin, moving at double time as her chest rose and fell faster, a rush of red desire creeping up from her breasts.

"And you're just stalling, my dear." The kiss was inevitable, the taste of her sealing the beat, a searing sense of closure that felt like an ending and a beginning all at once, joined in a circle of looping, blind want.

She returned his eagerness with full power, her hand sliding behind his back, fingers scrambling to unearth his skin, the not-so-gentle drag of her manicure against his spine like a stroke of his shaft. He groaned, his tongue tangled with hers, their breath coming together like their blood. Memory took him, swiftly, back to their first time together.

Kara broke the kiss, the sound of her breath rasping against his cheek like church bells in the distance, a song of happiness and hope. "I think you should know that I don't act like this on all my dates with men. I don't want you to get the wrong idea."

Her gaze was focused on him, her eyes hooded with lust. He knew if he reached between her legs he would find her wet. Pleasure was his goal. Giving her ecstasy, watching her relax and yield, giving him the tortured honor of touching her until she clung to him, then let him come inside her, their joining complete. Hot dreams had tormented him for so long, all that was left of their short time together, that he felt surreal in these unfolding seconds, as if he'd conjured her from a place of half-conscious desperation.

Cupping her breast, his fingers found her nipple, stroking it until her response was unquestioning.

No. She was real.

Her hand found his hard thigh, moving up with a growing sense of ownership that made his chest burst. Maddening. The woman was maddening.

Just then, the waiter appeared with the first course. Tablecloths and napkins obscured their hands, though Kara quickly brought hers up, grabbing the wineglass and downing its contents as if she were a desert wanderer, parched and needy. Lars followed her lead, legs tense, answers to the waiter's questions coming out in monosyllabic requirements until they were alone again.

"This looks good," Kara said, taking a bite of some salad meant to resemble a modern art painting, with geometrically carved slices of heirloom beets arranged around gold-colored slivers of root vegetables and rosemary sprigs.

As he realized she really planned to actually eat her meal, he pivoted, taking a deep breath through his nose, reaching for his salad fork. Four bites later, he was done.

And still hungry.

For her.

"You look good."

"Is that all we're going to talk about? How much you want me?"

"It's a captivating topic."

"Pick a different one."

"Let's talk about how you disappeared that morning nearly three years ago." The anger in him flared, indignation at years lost a layer of gasoline thrown onto the bonfire.

"Let's go back to the old topic."

"Too late." He poured them both a second glass of wine and moved away from her, giving them just enough room so he could face her. Body heat diminished, her scent changing to something tinged with fear and reluctance.

Aha. He was right. Had been right all along. She'd stayed away all these years for a reason.

Six

Kara trembled to see the challenge in his eyes. He was upset she'd disappeared after a one-night stand, but he didn't know the half of it. Or the half of one percent of it. She'd hidden her name, and she'd hidden herself, but she'd also hidden his baby.

If he found out about Jamie now . . . he'd hate her, really hate her. And she couldn't blame him.

But a man like him had received everything on a silver platter his entire life—family, fame, fortune, wealth, power, and good looks. He was free. He had no idea what it was like for people like her. She'd had nothing she hadn't grabbed and taken without asking permission. And in Jamie's case, hidden so that others—who already had everything—couldn't take him from her.

She could explain part of the truth, however; she owed him that.

"It never occurred to me you'd want to see me again," she said. "I thought you'd be glad I saved us both an awkward goodbye."

"Why wouldn't I want to see you again?" His tone was sharp as the blades cutting root vegetables into sculpture in the restaurant's kitchen.

"Come on, Lars," she said, forcing a laugh. She gestured at

him—taking in the broad shoulders and long legs and photogenic cheekbones, the thousand-dollar trousers and priceless diamond earring, the confident bearing, the air of entitlement so quickly confirmed by everyone he met. "You're a rich and famous rock star from a powerful family. And I'm . . ."

He waited, eyes narrowing. "Yes?" he asked, a low purr. "Who are you?"

"I'm none of those things." Anger came to her rescue this time, rushing through her veins and strengthening her spine. "I'm a nobody, which must be obvious to you. A tiger shifter wouldn't be serving drinks if she were part of your world. She would've gone to all the best boarding schools in Europe, vacationed in the same exotic places like Fiji and I don't know where, partied together at Hollywood charity balls so often we'd be like brother and sister—"

"Then how lucky for both of us that is not the case," he growled, reaching out and capturing her wrist. A fingertip caressed her racing pulse. "But it doesn't answer my question. Why hide? Why run? Is wealth and pleasure that repulsive to you?"

She let him hold her wrist for a moment, knowing she could make him release her with a few painful, well-aimed words.

He pulled her against his side. "Or is it me who you find so disgusting?"

Oh, as if. Even now she was fighting the urge to climb into his lap and lick him from head to toe. "You aren't known for your long-term relationships, Lars."

He didn't flinch. "Only because I hadn't met the right woman yet." He lifted her hand, turned it over, and dropped a featherlight kiss on the tender skin on the underside of her wrist.

It was what she wanted to hear, but how could she believe it?

They were the words that men had dished out since the dawn of time to get reluctant women to have sex with them.

"Your family has a different idea about what the right woman is. And so do your friends and everyone you know, probably. I was just being realistic. I had to protect myself." *And my son.*

"You mention my family," he said in a low voice. "But I think we both know who you mean. My mother was a very forceful, very . . . determined . . . woman who was eager for me and my brothers to find successful mates. She and my father were very happy together, you see. And keeping her opinions to herself and living quietly were never appealing to her. As painful as it is for me to admit this, she may have developed a reputation that could have reached even—" Here he cut himself off and kissed her wrist again.

"Even women like me." She pulled her arm free, reclaimed her wineglass, and brought it to her lips, hoping he didn't notice the way her hand shook. "You made my point for me. You know we could never be together."

"On the contrary. We've already proven that we're fantastic together." He grinned in a way that made her toes curl.

"Sex isn't enough." Ignoring her toes, she gave him a pointed stare. "Not for me. I'll never settle, Lars. Not for you, not for any man."

"I'm extremely glad to hear it," he said, still grinning.

Why was he . . . happy? He was supposed to turn and run away. Didn't he realize what she was telling him? She wasn't going to have sex with him because she wanted more. She wanted everything. Everything she couldn't have.

Her heart began pounding harder.

This was all wrong. He wasn't the man she'd thought he was.

A small voice whispered in her ear, *he's the man you'd hoped he was*, but she told that voice to shut up.

"I'm so glad we've cleared that up," Lars said, signaling to the waiter for the check.

"Where are we going?" she asked, hoping the powerful urges that made her wet were driving him mad as well. She quickly poked a piece of feta on her plate and popped it into her mouth to stave off starvation, then swallowed the rest of her wine hurriedly.

"I need to prove to you that this isn't just about sex." He threw a pile of money on the table and reached for her hand. Matching his step, she found herself practically dragged out of the restaurant. Turning to the left, he pulled her into a dark cove covered with a pergola, the latticework ceiling woven with grapevines and warm lights.

"How do you plan to do that?" she asked, breathing hard against his chest, unable to look up.

With whipcord strength, he seized her, the heat of his body, the pulse of his blood pounding into her as he nipped her earlobe, making her dizzy.

"With sex, of course."

"Here?" she gasped, the thrill of her words making him tremor slightly, as if all his need pooled at the end of each cell, trying to break through his skin. Each time he kissed her, Lars tasted wine, then a sweet, tangy flavor that reminded him of pussy.

Speaking of which, Lars bent at the knees, his mouth brushing against her pert nipple, his hand finding the top of her thigh, moving up to the wetness he knew would greet his fingertips. She moaned, low and deep, as his fingertip found her clit, the ripe pearl begging for his featherlight strokes.

"I thought," she choked out, "this wasn't just about sex." The final word came out like a murmur, a hoarse shout that told him she was close to climax. Reading her body, watching her respond to him in the dimly lit corner of the old brownstone where the restaurant resided, the sounds of traffic and the city behind them, made him want her more.

"It isn't," he said, hushed words in her ear as he slipped two fingers in her sweet warmth, his thumb grazing her clit as he moved his fingers inside her, Kara clutching his lapel in one shaking hand.

"Then what are you doing?" She closed her eyes, her legs beginning to quake, teeth trapping her bottom lip as she bit down, beginning to rock gently against his hand, seeking pleasure.

"Making sure that the part that *is* about sex is very much still there."

And with that, he took her mouth, knowing the orgasm would rock her as his tongue stroked the roof of her mouth, her moans gaining with the rhythm he set for her, the sound muted by his mouth against hers. Lars needed to capture all her energy, every drop of lust, each wave of ecstasy he made for her like reaching back in time to pull memory into the present.

The palpable *now*.

Kara tensed, trapping his hand between thighs of steel as she reached for his shoulder and bit him hard, her teeth nearly breaking through the wool of his jacket, her hips arching up to meet his hand. His cock strained against his trousers, the swollen pulse in his pants driving him into a madness as Kara released herself, the scent all pervading.

A beat began to align, his cock, heart, gut and soul all pulsing in a low, resonant tone. As he kissed her, he felt her heartbeat match his, the powerful pull of her blood rushing to meet him.

Not a beat.

The Beat.

He had to be in her, public be damned.

"Oh my God, Lars." She groaned as she shuddered against him, pressing harder, seeking more. Her eagerness sustained him.

What she did next emboldened him.

Kara unfastened his belt buckle, unzipping him, her hand sliding along the hard lines of his shaft.

He tipped into the frenzied wild, her leg up and around his hip, her thin panties torn off and flung into a small rosemary bush nearby as he plunged into her, the press of his forehead against hers, their mingled breath the only air he could breathe.

"Kara, you feel like home," he whispered, driving hard into her, all pretense long gone, his body hammering into her as she kissed him, openmouthed and making sounds that urged him on.

"More," she cried out in a hoarse voice. "Deeper. Come into me. Come in, come in, come in," she implored him, her hands everywhere, the shawl slipping from her shoulders to the ground beneath them as the heel of her shoe scratched against his leg, his climax rushing to the very tip of his soul.

The desperation pushed him further at the same time it shocked him. She shared it, matching him move for move, sigh for sigh, groan for groan as he spilled himself in her, Kara's core tightening from pelvis to neck, a remarkable show of strength and beauty that pulled his cock in like a lifeline. She rescued him in those seconds, buoyant and free, tethered and saved.

In return, she stifled screams against his shoulder, the bite finally breaking skin, the ferocity of her violent coming like an ancient ritual Lars didn't know existed, but one that made so much sense once revealed.

A deep truth.

A divine revelation.

A vibration that resonated through every cell, marking them as mates.

"I couldn't wait. Can't wait," he panted, the sound of his own breath a gritty noise, half groan and half sigh, the exertion of sex barely scratching the surface of how much of her body and soul he needed to possess. Lars' blood beat fast and slow, hot and cold, his entire physical state in disarray as she scattered him to the four corners of the universe at the same time that her tantalizing juices encased him in the finest, sexiest honey he ever wanted to taste.

He smelled her emotions, the pinpointing of the exact second when she moved from animal mind, out of sensation and into thought as her confusion and worry tinged her scent.

"You're more than I remembered, Kara," he said, reluctantly pulling out of her, reaching into his breast pocket to hand her a monogrammed handkerchief. She took it, staring uncomprehendingly, her cheeks bright pink, a slight glow of exertion dampening her hair along the edge of her face.

Discreetly he tucked himself back in, need rising up already. Insatiable, he suddenly existed only to touch her. To be with her.

But not here. His apartment was a far more civilized location for carnal pleasure.

"Nightcap? My place?" he asked, pulling her skirt down, caressing her smooth legs as she righted herself, giving him a look of unfettered desire. The question wasn't really about giving her a choice.

And she knew it.

"If this isn't just about sex, Lars, you have a funny way of showing it."

"Give me the night, and I'll show you everything you want."

She looked him up and down, clearly liking what she saw, her eyes going troubled at the pierced cloth of his shoulder where she'd bit him. Kara tapped her lips with her fingers as if chiding them.

"That's what I'm afraid of," she murmured.

He put one arm around her waist, guiding her to his waiting limo.

"Afraid of what I'll show you?"

Her tongue peeked out between bruised, raw lips.

"Afraid you really *will* show me everything I want."

"What does that mean?"

The half smile she gave him made a spark of electricity fly from his tailbone to the tip of his head. "Never mind. That nightcap sounds fabulous."

And with that, they were off to his apartment.

Where everything would be on the table.

Seven

Kara rested against his warm, strong body as the limo snaked through the Boston streets, listening to the beating of his heart. It seemed to thrum to the sound of her name. *Kara. Kara. Kara.*

"Excuse me, darling." He leaned away from her and reached into his pocket for his phone, which she belatedly realized had been chiming for some time. He stared at the screen for a moment, hesitating before he answered. "This is Lars."

She looked down at their intertwined hands and smiled. She could hear his heartbeat. His blended with hers, two notes in harmony: *Lars, Kara, Lars, Kara.*

They could be One. She wouldn't have believed they could have this together if she hadn't begun hearing the Beat at the moment of climax—and yeah, she knew that sounded like wishful thinking, but she'd never, ever felt anything like that before, even with him on That Night.

Lars. He was her One. Joy spiked through her like a drug. They had a child together, and she had to tell him as soon as possible. Tonight. If the legend was true . . .

It was true. It was. The truth was pounding so loudly in her ears she was deaf to the rest of the world.

Her mother hadn't been much of a parent, but she'd taught her a lot about the old ways. After her mother's trip to Europe with her father, she'd become obsessed with learning as much as she could, and everything she knew, legend or fiction or truth, she'd shared later with Kara. Kara's favorite of all the legends was that of the One. She'd always been a romantic and hated herself for it, but she couldn't stop herself from dreaming about a man born for her just as she was born for him, that the sound of their own hearts beating together—the Beat—would guide them to each other.

It was a dream she'd abandoned a long time ago when she'd given up on foolish dreams for herself to focus on realistic happiness for her child.

But now she was hearing the Beat. With Lars, Jamie's father. Whatever obstacles stood between them were irrelevant if they were born for each other. She had to see if she was right, tell him everything and trust her heart.

Trust the Beat.

"She *what?*" Lars asked. His voice had turned sharp, cold, dangerous.

His voice terrified her almost as much as the look in his eyes. He stared at her with such hate, such wounded betrayal, it could only mean one thing.

Her hands began to tremble. No, it was too soon. She had to be the one to tell him. If he heard it from somebody else, he'd never believe that she would've told her himself, that she was falling, had fallen—

"Tell me everything," he said, but not to her. Still listening to the voice on the phone. "Nevada, you say?"

No, he needed to hear it from her. Everything from her. Jamie had been born in Nevada, came a week early, the local emergency room at the hospital where she gave birth, terrified and alone. If Lars was talking about Nevada, then—

She reached out and splayed her fingers over his heart. "Lars, I need to tell you something."

He pushed her hand aside and held up a finger between them, eyes blazing. A chill washed over her.

Nobody's heart seemed to be beating anymore.

"Repeat the date of birth," he spat out.

"Let me explain," she said, but in growing despair, she realized it was too late. The bond that had formed between them over the past few hours had opened up his soul to her, making the hatred washing over him now as clear to her as if it were her own.

He would never forgive her for this. She'd never forgive herself.

Oh God. *They* knew about Jamie. Maybe whoever was on the phone was there right now with Jamie, with Nana, scaring them, taking them away.

All thoughts of the Beat and idiotic pink-princess dreams of her tiger prince rescuing her vanished in a heartbeat. A single heartbeat: her own. As it should be. As it had always been.

"Take me home," she said, using the bitchy, tough voice she reserved for drunk men with wandering hands. *"Now."* She couldn't afford to wallow in self-loathing right now. All she could think of was how she had to get home to her baby.

"A child?" he choked out. As their eyes locked, she saw the kind of raw, ferocious pain she'd feared. The kind of pain she'd felt at the idea of losing Jamie.

And she had inflicted it on Lars.

As quickly as his wounded, aching look had taken over his face, he tamped it down, the change in expression extraordinary.

His gaze drifted over her with contempt as he shoved his phone into his pocket. "You certainly played me like a master." One golden eyebrow arched. "Or should I say, 'pro'? When were you going to start attempting to extract payment for the little brat?"

What did he call Jamie? His own son? What kind of monster . . ."I tried to avoid you," she said. "You pursued me. You insisted."

"You certainly wanted me to feel like it was all my idea," he said. He winced. "A child. Congratulations. I fell for it. Every blush, every sigh, every giggle. Like a damn fool."

"I don't giggle."

"Not when you're yourself, I don't imagine, only when you're pretending to be a poor little waitress. Tell me, Kara, are you hoping tonight is as profitable for you as our first evening together?"

The man she'd thought he was—the man she'd fooled herself into believing was her One, God how embarrassing—was really an entitled, arrogant buttwipe. She hated him. Claws hardened under her fingertips, straining to break through her soft human skin and tear his face off.

"Take. Me. Home." Her voice rumbled with her emerging tiger's growl.

"Home," he scoffed. "Right. You really had me there. As if a woman like you would be living in a slum like that. To think . . ." He made a disgusted sound and turned away from her.

"It's not a slum. Rich assholes like you think everything except the Ritz is a slum."

"Oh, come on. Where do you *really* live? Who are you really?" His voice went deep with emotion, the sound like a long, slow scratch on the surface of her heart. "What kind of woman does this?" Just as fast as he showed his real feelings, his face closed up, twisting with a sneer.

Giving up on the spoiled weretiger, she crawled over to the driver's window and knocked on the opaque plexiglass. "Driver, take me home or let me out at the corner," she shouted.

The driver's voice came over the speaker. "Sir?"

Lars scoffed again. He pressed a button. "Drive to the lady's humble abode, as she insists."

"Asswipe," she muttered.

"Angel," he mocked sweetly. "I can't believe I fell for it. You're probably going to tell me now that the kid's actually mine. You think I'm going to beg you to let me see him? Were you hoping I'd be so eager to be a dad that I'd write you a big check and take him off your hands?" Those eyes, though. His words were weapons, but she knew she'd hurt him deeply. How could she feel so much at the same time? Too many contradictory feelings fought for dominance inside her.

"No," she spat out. Her teeth were getting too sharp to speak. She hadn't been this upset in a long, long time. If the driver didn't hurry, she was going to tear out of the limo as a full-formed tiger.

"Be quiet," he said dismissively. "I don't want to hear another word. If you're playing me, you need to be shut down." He frowned. "And if you really did bear my child, then you . . ." The sigh he let out filled her with a fierce shame and a defensive independence that turned into a low roar in her throat.

She dug her claws—they were out now, curling and sharp—into the leather seat, and focused all her energy on stopping the rest of the shift. The dress was straining at the zipper, but she was able to maintain her womanly shape except for the claws. And the teeth.

He didn't want to hear another word? He didn't want to be a

father? He thought she was a whore?

Good. Then he'd never want to see her again.

She was free of him. She would raise Jamie to be a better man.

The struggle to contain her form and her rage made the ride to her apartment a slow agony, but eventually they pulled up outside her building and the driver got out, walked back, and opened her door.

Lars looked as if he was struggling for control himself. His blue eyes had turned golden—from sky to sun. And they burned just as hot.

If he didn't want to be a father, they would never see each other again.

Good.

"He's not yours," she said, her voice not entirely human. With a sneer, she turned to the door. "He's much too good to be yours."

And then, discarding the fight against her own nature, she leapt out of the car, landing gracefully on the sidewalk on all four of her sleek, ginger paws.

Fuck her.

Lars felt the change creep over him, no surprise as emotions surged through him like a solar flare, too much to contain in any mere human body. As Kara had begun her own shift, the contagion struck him to the core, fueled by betrayal, fury, and pure disgust.

She had a child. A two-year-old. A little boy she had hidden from him. The birth date was so close. *Too* close. The child could be his.

His.

With her juices still coating his fingers, their mingled sex scent radiating from his cock, he felt the world shimmer, melting and surreal. A baby. A boy. She had a child.

What else had she lied about?

The flash of hurt as his associate had blurted out the news made him want to hurt *her*, pierce her heart, shatter her world into a million shards of gasping incredulity to match how he felt.

All that beauty, all that haunting memory converged in these hours together, a blend of past and present that guaranteed a blissful future. He'd set aside every hesitation for her, the wind knocked out of him by the powerful impact of certainty, her response to his presence, his touch, his frenzied sexual power so clear.

And yet . . .

She'd lied to him. All these years, the mystery woman he'd yearned for had avoided him because—

Because what? Why? If the child was the spawn of another man—or worse, another shifter—then Lars was one of a string of men she'd fucked in that same timeframe. What he had thought was special was cheap. Tawdry.

Nothing more than being played by a woman with no morals.

The kind of woman his late mother had always warned him about.

And if the child *was* his, somehow that was worse. Worse than being a fuckstick for a whore. He flinched at the word, hating to hold it in his mind with an image of Kara. In the end, he couldn't, his hands raking through his hair, his fists pounding on his thighs as emotion took over, every thought turning to shredded confetti in a wind tunnel.

The mystery woman he had obsessed over for years had deprived him of his right to nurture and raise and love his own progeny. His heir.

His *son*.

James Woodside Jablonski was his name.

Woodside. That was the name of the estate where the party three years ago had been held. Could it mean he really was the baby's father? Hope blossomed inside, growing, taking over.

Or did it mean she'd slept with more than one man that night?

Damn it. Anger filled his deflated soul.

Tapping his phone, he reached Don, his associate. "I need a family law lawyer. The best."

"Yes, sir. The one Mrs. Jensen retained?"

The mention of his mother's name jarred him. "Yes. What-ever," he snapped. "I need paternity testing and custody papers by sunlight."

"Indeed, sir. I'll start the process immediately. He has experience with paternity testing and the family."

"He . . . what?"

Don went silent, clearly debating what to say. "Your mother experienced this with one of your brothers."

Surprise turned to fury, a rippling grief that choked him. With Mother dead, he couldn't ask. And time was of the essence, so trying to track down his brothers would be futile. Lars practically flung the phone out the window, so angered, his stomach sour, neck tight.

Swirling thoughts made him numb, then hot, then boiling, then ice as his animal mind fought to take over. Vision sharpened. Scents overpowered him. The leather seat felt like dead prey, limp and cool, mocking him.

Like Kara.

Played for a fool, he knew his reaction was over the top, yet he felt the exaggeration as it oozed over the surface of his heart. She had lied about one of the most primitive and intense instincts.

Breeding.

He's not yours, she had said, the words a weapon. Not truth. Not necessarily, at least. Paternity testing would be required, a formality in a lab.

Kara would have no choice.

Deprived of the truth, and slapped in the face with it now after years of deception, he felt rocked into combat mode, on edge, fighting for his life.

Fighting for his heart.

He released his shoulders and let the shift take him, needing the inevitable pain that came with bones that elongated and crackled, with tendons accustomed to drumsticks that turned into paws. His jaw ached as it stretched, sharp teeth narrowing and growing, the pressure of his nose as it widened and went wet a familiar, orderly sensation. Pushing against the back of the driver's seat, he felt too caged by the limo.

Fumbling for the window switch, barely able to think in human mode, he found himself stymied by his driver, who merely said, "Two blocks, sir. Two blocks to safety."

The low purr turned into a roar of outrage, a jaw-popping movement that made him feel worse and better. Lars' long claws scraped against the door, his tiger face clear in the limo's rearview mirror. A blank expression greeted him.

No emotion.

By the time he leapt from the car into a wooded area and began to sprint, dodging trees as his paws dug into the decayed leaves and topsoil, his feet enjoying the swift rise and fall of his growing gait, he only knew the sheer freedom of the loping run that took him away from Kara's scent.

And toward the one place in Boston where he knew he would be safe.

Eight

Kara had been unable to enter her apartment as a tiger, so she'd hidden in an alley and calmed down before she shifted back into her human form. Then she'd had to dig through her ripped clothes for her phone.

"Hi, it's Kara," she said when Nana answered. "Code orange."

Nana didn't waste time. "Where?"

"Behind the dumpster in the alley, west of the front door."

"Right downstairs?"

"Yes."

Nana hung up without another word, and in less time than Kara thought possible for the elderly woman, there she was with a change of clothes.

Kara grabbed them, pulled on the sweatpants and T-shirt, then threw her arms around her rescuer for a thankful squeeze.

Nana held up her arm to reveal a pair of flip-flops dangling from her fingers. "In case you can't find those heels."

Kara hugged her again. "Nana, you're a miracle. You think of everything." Hopping on one foot, she put on the sandals and took Nana's arm as they returned up to the apartment.

"I can smell him on you," Nana said cheerfully. "I hope you had a good time."

"You found me naked in an alley. You think I had a good time?"

Nana stopped just inside the apartment and gave her a chiding look. "Could be. Cats often enjoy themselves in a dark alley."

Kara closed her eyes, the flush of anger draining out of her, leaving only pain. "I'm sorry. I shouldn't have snapped at you. I'm so, so grateful you were here to help me."

"It's a good thing you made it so close to home before shifting," Nana said. "I wouldn't have been able to leave Jamie otherwise. He would've had to come with me, and you know how he hates having his sleep interrupted."

Kara looked around the apartment for any sign of invasion or disturbance. "Did anyone come by tonight?"

"Who's going to come by?"

Kara dead bolted and chained the door. "Anybody call?"

"Nobody. It's been very quiet. Except for that baby, of course. He yowled like crazy when I tried to trim those claws of his."

"Claws?" Kara grabbed Nana by the shoulders. "Did he . . ." At two, Jamie was overdue for a complete shift into his tiger form. If she'd had more money, she could've consulted a shifter doctor, but such professionals were rare, if she even knew where to find one, and she would need thousands of dollars just for the consultation.

"No, sorry, dear, I was just being colorful. His toenails had gotten deadly. But I took care of them."

Kara let out her breath. So much to worry about, so much to plan, so much to do. They had to get out of the city, out of the state. Start over. "Nana, we have to change our names. Do you know anybody who can help us do that?"

"Kind of late for that, isn't it sweetheart?"

Kara combed her fingers through her hair, as tangled as it

usually was after a shift. "If only I'd done it two years ago. I just didn't think I'd ever see him again, or that he'd care . . ."

"He found out about Jamie, did he?" Nana asked.

"He's horrible and thinks I want his money, and I never want to see him again."

Nana made a noncommittal grunt.

Kara went on. "He accused me of being a slut who got pregnant on purpose, maybe not even with him!"

"I imagine he was quite upset to learn there was a child," Nana said.

As hard as she tried, Kara couldn't maintain her rage. Instead, she felt tears start to burn in her eyes. She buried her face in her hands. "He hates me."

"I doubt that, sweetheart."

"I heard the Beat and thought he was the One, and now he hates me."

"If he's the One, he certainly doesn't hate you," Nana said.

"He's not the One."

"That's a shame," Nana said. "I made cookies while you were out. Chocolate chip. How about we—"

"First thing in the morning we have to find somebody who can help get us fake IDs," Kara said.

"You're just going to run away?"

"You know the Jensens! How do you think he found out about Jamie so fast? They have people who can do anything."

"I always thought that maybe you didn't change your name because you were kind of hoping he would find you," Nana said.

"What?"

"Poor man wouldn't have had a chance if you'd really tried to hide from him," Nana said. "You wanted to be sporting."

"No, that's not—"

"And you must've liked him an awful lot to have sex with him that night. And then to have his baby."

"Nana! You're suggesting I wanted all of this to happen?"

"Yes, that's exactly what I'm suggesting."

Kara gaped at her. "No. It's not true."

Was it?

Muttering to herself that it was impossible, she checked on Jamie and then went to the bathroom to clear her head, turning on the shower as an afterthought. The aches from the shift were still with her, her body tasted like *him*, and her thoughts were fuzzy with cat brain. Not to mention sex brain.

Could she have really wanted him to find her?

As she lathered up the soap and arched under the hot spray, she imagined his face the night they'd met. In spite of herself, she smiled. If he'd been the man she'd hoped he was, then yes, she'd wanted him to find her. *If* he'd wanted to find her again, she wanted him to have a chance. Sporting, as Nana had said.

How hard could he have searched if he'd only run into her accidentally—now when he was here on business? Not very hard.

Her smile vanished. He hadn't really cared enough to find her.

What should her new name be? She ran through a list in her mind but was miserable with all of them. When she got out of the shower, she dressed in black leggings and a black sweater, feeling as grim and hopeless as she ever had.

She'd never been in such terrible danger of losing Jamie. The stress, the worry, the fear of Lars taking him from her would kill her if it went on. How could she live day after day, year after year under such a threat?

She returned to Jamie's crib and watched him sleep. Curled

up on one side, he clutched a stuffed baby tiger, a gift Kara had bought the day she'd found out she was pregnant.

Life on the run wasn't possible. It would be bad for her, but more importantly, it would be bad for Jamie.

The only thing to do was stand and fight.

⸻

"Fight her, damn it!" Lars yelled into the phone as he finished dressing in one of the Novo Club rooms, pants on and unfastened, his clean shirts hanging on a small butler serving caddy as he paced nervously around the stone-walled room, fuming. His shift last night had been a grave error. The news channels were filled with lurid tales of a wild tiger on Newbury Street, terrorizing the streets of Boston. Morgan had gracefully brought a small television into his quarters so he could monitor the morning news situation.

But none of that mattered. His lawyer was on the phone, and Lars was determined.

"Sir, we can't draw up custody papers so quickly. We'll need until midafternoon, possibly tomorrow morning, to complete the process, and even that would be an expedited process."

"I don't want to hear the word 'can't.'"

"You don't know that the child is yours."

"Then do whatever legal maneuvers we need to perform to find out! I want an answer within twenty-four hours." Lars threw his phone across the room, the shatter of glass against stone satisfying for about two seconds. He was close to punching the wall, his blood still settling back into his human form, his legs so full of impulse he began jumping in place to push out energy.

A pull-up bar attached to the wall provided some relief as he grabbed it. Five chin-ups in, he felt his shoulder blades turn from rock to molten lava, the fury bleeding out his pores as he exerted himself. Ten pull-ups and his triceps groaned, but he ignored them.

As long as the thought of her betrayal could be shoved aside by any means necessary—including destroying his arms—Lars would take it.

Why? Why, why, *why* hadn't she told him about the baby? Was the little boy his? Did he really have a son—and with his mystery woman? Reeling at the thought, he punished himself, the pull-ups harder to execute, the challenge welcomed by his frantic mind. Anything to focus on.

Anything.

When he could pull his chin to the bar no longer, he dropped to the floor, agile and prowling, grabbing a T-shirt and throwing it on, fastening his pants as an afterthought. The old guard in the shifter world demanded a dress code for the Novo Club, but not in the fitness center. He needed to lift.

He needed to make his blood burn with anything but the thought of her touch.

As Lars padded out into the hallway, running an angry, throbbing hand through his thick hair, Morgan appeared, a shadow on wheels.

"New telephone, sir?"

"Yes. And a drum set."

A discreet nod. That was all it took. Morgan knew.

The club's fitness center was small but enough. Free weights, a few machines, a small saltwater pool, and a bear.

Yes, a bear.

"Lars!" Derry boomed, giving him a smile. The man held a three-hundred-pound barbell in one hand. "I take it you're here to spot me?"

"Shove your jovial bullshit up your ass, Derry. Give me that."

"Ah, and a fine day to you too, sir." Derry handed over the barbell as if it were a broom. Lars grunted with the effort of the exchange, propelled by the blinding horror of what Kara had done to him, sorrow for lost time swapping quickly with outrage.

"I may have a child!" he blurted out. "A fucking child. One I've been kept from. Either I've been fooled, or I've been suckered."

"Lars, you may be many things, but a sucker and a fool aren't two of them."

Lars grabbed a second barbell, adjusted the weights accordingly, and began lifting, one after the other, rotating his elbows and wrists in a pattern that soon soothed him as much as it exhausted him. He needed to drive her out of his blood.

No matter how many rhythms he tried, she would not leave.

The Beat remained.

Changing positions, he sat on a lifting bench and reclined, balancing the barbells above him, working his lats and pecs. Derry stared at him, drinking a sports drink, the bright label out of place in this fitness center, itself paradoxical in the cavernous, nineteenth-century haven that shifters two generations ago had built as a safe house.

"Fucking beat," Lars muttered.

"I'm beat too. Bored as well. Jessica and her sister are upstairs with Molly picking out clothing for some charity event."

Lars remembered his manners. Barely. "How"—grunt—"goes your wedding planning?"

"Wedding planning? I'm a prop in my own wedding, I assure you. If they could miniaturize me and turn me into a cake topper, they would." Derry smiled to himself, then frowned. "Me, about to be married. Can you believe it?"

"Me, a father. Can you believe it?" Lars mimicked.

"Are you certain? That the baby is yours?"

"No."

"Then why torture yourself until you know?"

The drumbeat wouldn't stop. Even as Kara had fled the limo last night, it had roared on. Even as he'd shifted and wandered the streets in tiger form, it had been a sonorous companion, his heartbeat amplified to something godlike.

"Because I know," Lars confessed, racking the barbells, slamming the metal around as if it were a pillow. He paced, heedless of his formal dress pants, sweat soaking his shirt. He was a mess. He knew it.

"How?"

If he said it, Derry would take him for a fool. The Beat was old legend, the stuff of fairies and wood nymphs. No one believed that shit these days, right?

Might as well admit to being anally probed by aliens in the desert.

"I just . . . The dates line up."

Derry gave him a stern look, sniffing elegantly. "You're a terrible liar, Lars. Always have been. Even when we were kids."

Buh-BOOM! Buh-BOOM!

The Beat grew louder within, making him slide against the wall, down on his ass, knees up, elbows resting on them as he ran his fingers through his sweat-soaked hair. "Jesus, Derry, I'm going crazy. I need a drum set. I need to bang on something."

"How about a lovely filly from the Plat? I'm sure you could bang on—"

"I can't stop this fucking beat." Allowing himself to just breathe, giving in to the pain of what Kara had done, he felt his heart melt as the beat continued.

"Beat?" Lars expected mirth in his tone, but his friend just stared at him.

"I know. I'm crazy, right? But I felt it with her three years ago. I had no idea what it was, but—"

A beefy hand the size of a dinner plate covered his shoulder. "I do understand. Every pounding revelation of it." Kind blue eyes, a deeper shade of blue than Lars' own, met his. "Why do you think I'm marrying Jessica?"

"I didn't realize," Lars said softly. "It's hard enough to believe, but . . . with a *human*?"

"Don't look at me like that! Gavin has it with Lilah too."

"I'm just . . . wow." Lars let his head sink down, resting his forehead on his knees. "I thought it was only a shifter legend. That only two shifters could feel it."

Derry shrugged. "It's more complicated than that."

"Isn't everything?"

Derry's phone buzzed. He looked at the screen, bushy eyebrows flying up in surprise. Turning his screen toward Lars, he said, "Giant tiger loose on Newbury Street? Seriously, Lars?"

He shrugged. "I couldn't help it." Lars sighed. "My father is going to kill me."

"Expect a reprimand from Asher, too. He's declared himself head of the shifter world these days." Derry pressed the play button on a video.

Our news team caught footage of the Siberian tiger, shown here as it sprints across traffic, headed for Boston common. Animal control specialists say the tiger found its way to the Charles River and disappeared. Exotic animal ownership has led to . . .

"Exotic animal, eh? When bear shifters get spotted in cities, we're usually found near dumpsters, so they call us trash eaters, starvation pushing us into the cities." Derry's face made it clear he'd prefer to be called an exotic animal.

"We all have our crosses to bear," Lars said.

Derry groaned.

"How do you get rid of it?" Lars asked.

"Get rid of what?"

"This damned beat. It feels like it's in me. I can't make it go away."

"Why would you want to?"

"Because she betrayed me! Because she lied and—" Lars broke off the rant as he looked up to find Derry frowning at him.

"Maybe you are a fool," Derry muttered.

"What?"

"Lars. Buddy. You can't get rid of The Beat. Ever. You have it for a reason."

"WHAT?"

"You can't make it go away."

"But she—But I—But . . . oh, fuck," he gasped, Derry's words sinking in.

Derry closed his eyes and sighed. "There's your answer. You're feeling The Beat because she's yours. Yours forever. She's your One."

Lars began to laugh, a strange sound of joy and pain that he could never, ever replicate if asked. "This is ridiculous!"

Derry shrugged. "Welcome to the club."

Nine

Having decided to stand and fight for herself and her son, Kara vowed to live her life as if she hadn't been interrupted by any man, tiger, or Beat. She got as much sleep as she could, all things considered, then got up at her usual time and dressed in jeans for a day of playing with Jamie. Later she would put on a dress and heels for her early evening shift at the Plat. As nervous as it made her, she'd decided to face the music, and she would.

As she slipped her feet into a pair of black boots, she tried to ignore the sensation that her heartbeat had a twin. When she pulled up the zipper over her calf, she could hear it thrumming in her chest, inside her, around her. An echo, as if their souls were holding hands.

"Pretend it's indigestion," she muttered to herself. She popped an antacid into her mouth and marched to the kitchen to make herself ginger tea.

But it wasn't Kara who needed TLC. Nana sat at the table with her hand over her heart, her wide-eyed gaze fixed on nothing.

"Nana!"

"Oh, hi. You're up already?" Nana asked vaguely, blinking a few times.

"What's wrong?" Kara squatted next to her and held her hands. They felt bony, delicate, and too cold. "Something's wrong."

"I have this pain," Nana said with a sigh. "It's probably nothing."

"Where?" Kara's throat tightened. Nothing bad could happen to Nana. It just couldn't.

"Oh, I'm sure it's nothing."

Kara squeezed Nana's hands. "We're going to the doctor."

"What doctor? I don't have a doctor. I hate doctors."

"Then we'll go to the emergency room." Kara jumped up, stroking Nana's shoulder. "You stay right there and rest for a minute while I get ready."

"I'm not going anywhere unless you make me."

Kara was going to make her. Nana had spent her life taking care of other people; Kara had to do the same for her. Within five minutes, she had Jamie on her hip, his diaper bag on her shoulder, and Nana on her arm.

"I'm fine," Nana said, shaking off her support. "Really, I was just dizzy for a second. And I've got gas. Really, I'm fine."

"Let's hear the doctor say it. Please, Nan? Otherwise I'll be worrying myself sick about you."

"Oh, fine. For you then." Nana strode ahead of her down the stairs, but Kara noticed she gripped the handrail tightly.

Out on the street, Nana started to walk toward the bus stop when Kara restrained her. "We've got an Uber coming."

"Don't waste your money," Nana said. "I'll be fine on the bus—"

Kara pointed at the man driving up to the curb. "Here he is. This blue Toyota."

"But what about Jamie's car seat?" Nana started to go back

to the apartment, then paused and pressed her fist against her stomach, a grimace on her face.

Alarmed, Kara ushered Nana inside the car. "There's a car seat, see?"

The driver looked worried about taking a sick old lady to the hospital, but Kara told him they were visiting a sick friend, not actually about to die in his car themselves, and soon they were pulling up to Mount Auburn Hospital.

And then, two hours later, after the doctor told Nana they were concerned about her heart, she was admitted for overnight observation.

"See?" Kara said, tucking the thin hospital blanket around Nana's hips.

"Thee?" Jamie said, reaching for the blinking lights on Nana's electronic monitor.

Nana crossed her arms over her chest, jutting out her chin, but her eyes were half-closed and her voice was weak. "This is going to cost a fortune. I don't need all this fuss. Really, Kara, this is totally ridiculous. You get that baby out of here before he catches something serious."

Kara pulled Jamie away from another machine and lifted him into her arms. If only she could bring Jamie to a friend or sitter and come back to be with Nana—but she didn't have a friend or a sitter, and she was due at work in less than an hour. "Don't worry about the bills. Life comes first."

"I'll be fine. You go and take that baby out of this germy place, will you?"

"Call me if anything—"

"Go," Nana said.

Telling herself she'd call the hospital every hour, Kara brought

Jamie home, well slathered with hand sanitizer, and began to panic about how she could serve drinks at the Platinum Club with a toddler at her side. When she couldn't think of any solution, she called Eva.

"Bring him," Eva said. "Molly would love to watch him."

"Molly?"

"She used to work for me. Now she works for herself. Runs a boutique in the building, engaged to Edward Stanton. You'll love her, she'll love you. I'll tell her you're coming."

"But—but—shouldn't you ask her first?"

"I'll talk to her now, but I know Molly. She and Jess would love to take care of a baby. They might play with him a little too much, actually—I hope you don't mind if he stays up late."

"Jess? Isn't that . . ."

"The one engaged to Derry Stanton. She also worked for me. Friends with Molly. You bring Jamie to my office, and the girls will be waiting for you here. The Plat is like a family sometimes." Eva cleared her throat. "Especially when I'm short a waitress and can't afford to have another one of you miss her shift."

"Got it," Kara said. "Thank you. We'll be there."

And so it was that Kara walked off the service elevator behind the Platinum Club with Jamie in his stroller and a diaper bag loaded with snacks and toys. As promised, Eva waited in her office with two very friendly looking women, Molly and Jess, and Kara felt her panic begin to ease.

"Oh my God," Jess said, beaming at Jamie. "He is so f—I mean, so darn cute!"

Molly, a round-faced brunette with blue eyes, sat on the floor and reached out to Jamie, a warm and nonthreatening gesture that won him over instantly.

"You're sure this is OK with you two?" Kara asked. "And Eva? You don't mind how I'll have to clock out a little early?"

"As long as you're working for the next four hours, we'll be fine," Eva said.

"My boutique is closed right now, so he can run around and have fun," Molly said. "Plus I've got a big-screen TV. And cheese crackers."

"He'll fall asleep in an hour," Kara said. "You'll probably get bored, honestly. Thank you, thank you, thank you—"

"Better get going," Eva said. "Carl just called me; they're swamped."

With a final kiss on Jamie's chubby cheek, Kara thanked them all again, waved, and headed out to the lounge.

Very rarely did Lars Jensen meet his match in a fitness club, but with Derry Stanton on the other end of the long, thick ropes, pumping in a rhythmic motion designed to produce endless sine waves, Lars could quite literally feel his arms turn into wet noodles.

Killing time in the Novo Club was a fool's errand, but he didn't care. No band performances were scheduled for the day. Waiting for his lawyer to call with news about Kara and the baby—no, toddler—meant certain irritation, the near-painful waiting making him a live wire.

Might as well abuse himself.

"Harder!" Derry shouted, not even breaking a sweat, grinning like a madman.

Challenge accepted. Lars pushed up with his legs, leveraging his strength from heels to hips, pushing his arms harder and harder until he realized, to his great horror, that he'd developed a new heartbeat.

Not a new rhythm.

An utterly new heartbeat independent of his own.

Startled, he dropped the ropes, one raking across his calf. Barely feeling the burn, he stumbled to the water cooler in a haze. Dehydration must be the cause. That's it. He poured water into his bottle and guzzled it, not caring as it spilled out the corners of his mouth, soaking the neck of his shirt, trickling down his chest, pooling under his navel and soaking into the fabric of his pants.

And still the new beat went on.

It was a flutter, a hiccup, an echo.

A figment of his imagination.

A medicine ball thwacked him square in the stomach, his involuntary *oof!* making Derry laugh.

"You're much more fun to work out with than any of my own brothers," he said, handing Lars a towel.

Lars kicked the medicine ball away from him. It barely moved, heavy with intent. "Why?"

"'Work out' might be a bit trendy," Derry said with a laugh. "It's not as if most shifters need to use equipment like this."

"But we can't all shift regularly and run wild in Montana," Lars noted. "Some shifters need to exercise the human way."

He made a derisive sound.

"Most shifters need to be careful with their animal state, especially in a city like Boston," Lars elaborated.

Derry looked at the television across the room, sound off but images flickering.

"Case in point," he said, droll and dry, as Lars' tiger form filled the screen.

"I was careless."

"You were distracted."

The flutter in his chest turned to raindrops on a tin drum. Lars coughed twice to chase it away. No luck.

A sudden pang of yearning for Kara nearly doubled him over, filled with a breathful of grief that tasted like her kisses. He reeled, staring uncomprehendingly at a worried Derry, who frowned.

"Lars?"

"This damned beat!" Throwing the towel aside, Lars picked up the medicine ball and tossed it at Derry, who caught it one-handed.

"It's not going away."

"Does it have to appear twice?" Pounding his chest once, he took a deep breath, willing it away. Every brush of his fingertips against his own skin reminded him of her. As he inhaled, he smelled her, the fresh tang of her arousal, the sweet relief of her tongue tangling with his.

The cool, flat softness of her palm against the back of his neck.

He despised himself for wanting her so much.

Hated her for betraying him.

Yet his true fury was reserved for his self-betrayal, for he questioned his own actions yesterday, wondering if he'd made a mistake. Pride goeth before a fall.

Was he being a prideful fool?

"Twice?" Derry's eyes narrowed with suspicion. "Lars? What do you mean, twice?"

"The double beat. The little one that comes immediately after the bigger one."

Long black hair brushed lightly against Derry's shoulders as he shook his head. "I don't know what you're talking about." Known for his jocularity and inability to remain serious in any given situation, Derry's expression made it clear he wasn't joking now.

Adrenaline kicked up a notch inside Lars' blood.

"The Beat! The One! You said so yourself!"

"But that's just it, Lars. It's *The* Beat. *The* One. Not two beats. Not two."

As the man's words registered, Lars closed his eyes, his inner world telescoping to a single sound, the out-of-sync beats that came in twos, one stronger than the other, lighter sound almost trying to catch up to the deeper, stronger heartbeat.

It grew stronger.

Stronger.

And then suddenly Lars sprinted out of the fitness room, Derry calling out his name as he raced up the stairs barefoot, ignoring everything but that second beat.

Which grew and grew and *grew* as he climbed floor by floor, a beacon that called him, a siren call he had no choice but to answer.

His blood.

Ten

Halfway through her shift, Kara called Nana at the hospital.

"Dehydration!" Nana cried. "Can you believe that? I get a little thirsty, and they insist on putting me in the hospital. I told them I want to go home, but they're keeping me until the morning. I've still got tubes sticking out of me."

"So your heart is all right?"

"As good as a woman half my age, the doctor said." Nana lowered her voice. "And they don't have any idea how old I really am."

"I'm so relieved, Nana."

"Yes, me too," Nana said grudgingly. "I suppose it's good to find out I've got to take care of myself a little better."

"I'll take care of you a lot better, too," Kara said.

Nana yawned loudly into the phone. "You need anything else? I'm going to catch some sleep before those nurses come back with their needles."

"I'll be there first thing in the morning."

"I'm not going anywhere. Take your time." She yawned again and ended the call.

Just as Kara was putting her phone in her pocket, she looked up at the TV over the bar.

"Oh my God," she whispered.

"I know, right?" replied the other waitress, a small woman with a platinum-blonde pixie cut. Kara could never remember her real name, but everyone called her Bell, short for Tinker Bell. "I can't believe they let people have tigers as pets, you know? And then they get out and eat people. Or, you know, scare them to death."

"Is this . . . *live*?" Kara asked. He could be in danger. People like Bell would panic, might even shoot him. She stared at the sleek, powerful cat on the screen. She'd never seen him as a tiger. He looked so . . .

Good. Familiar. Beautiful.

The echo in her heart pounded louder, drowning out Bell's words. She moved closer to the bar so she could read the words at the bottom of the screen. It had been recorded last night, and they hadn't found, caught, or harmed the animal.

Her animal.

Oh, oh, oh. She put a hand on the bar for support.

"Are you all right?" Carl asked.

In a daze, she looked over at the nice bartender. "I just need a little break."

Deafened by heartbeats, she didn't hear Carl's exact words, but he was gesturing for her to go.

After setting her tray and apron on the bar, she hurried across the lounge to the elevator and took the car up to Molly's boutique. She had to see Jamie. The world was such a dangerous place for shifters, and for exotic beings like weretigers in particular. Her mother had drilled it into her from the time she was in diapers that her animal shape could get her killed. As fun as it was to turn into a tiger in the first grade—other kids thought it was pretty cool—she could get herself, and her family, into deep, horrible trouble.

Seeing Lars on the TV had filled her with an urgent need to hold her baby, just for a minute, and then she could go back to work. She got off the elevator at the top floor—not bad for a fashion boutique—and saw an engraved gold plate on the wall directing her to Molly's.

She walked through a nondescript door into a small but luxurious penthouse suite on the eastern side of the building. The incredible view of the Charles River through the panoramic windows almost distracted her from her goal. But then she heard Jamie's familiar laughter and spun to catch him just as he leapt into her arms.

Molly waved from her seat on the couch, where she held one of Jamie's board books. Jess was there too, holding a juice box and the toy tiger.

"Mommy!" he cried.

"Hello, baby, how are you doing?" Kara buried her nose in his neck, inhaled his soft, perfect scent. Ah, yes. This was what she'd needed. Just a cuddle with her little guy. She heard the radio playing somewhere nearby, perhaps with the music she'd put in the diaper bag.

"Daddy!" he cried, twisting in her arms.

She sucked in a sudden, panicked breath. Lars? Could he be here? Had he tracked Jamie down through Eva? Or had Molly or Jess—

But then she realized Jamie was pointing at a TV. It was angled away from her, so she hadn't seen it. What she'd thought was the radio was the news that had been playing downstairs.

"Daddy on TV," Jamie said, bouncing in her arms so violently that she had to let him down to the floor. He ran around the sofa and slapped the expensive-looking television with both sticky palms, as if he were high-fiving the tiger that was loping across the screen.

Oh. My. God. She flushed, afraid to meet Molly or Jess's gaze. What must they think? How much did they know about shifters? They were each marrying a Stanton, so they must know something. Would they realize what it meant to have a child recognize the identity of a weretiger?

The implications made her knees weak. Not only had he recognized Lars as the weretiger, he'd recognized Lars as his father.

It was true, but Molly and Jess didn't need to know that. "You know about . . . ," Kara began, trailing off and making a vague gesture with her hand.

"Shifters?" Jess asked. "Oh yeah. We know." She gave Molly a funny smile.

"Good," Kara said. "OK. See, I shift into . . ." She gestured at the screen. Then the stuffed tiger in Jess's hands.

"You're a tiger shifter," Molly said, then added, "Like Jamie."

Kara gasped. "Did Eva tell—"

"Oh, no," Molly said. "I can see it. I'm not a shifter, but I . . . I can see things. I didn't want you to think Eva broke your confidence or that you have to worry about us sharing your secret."

"Was that you, Kara?" Jess asked, pointing at the screen.

"No, no. But I think Jamie's confused." Kara silently apologized to her little boy for accusing him of such a thing.

"Is he . . . Has he . . . ," Jess began.

"He hasn't shifted yet," Kara said softly, then bit her lip, fighting the tears pricking her eyes. It had been a long day.

"Is that bad?" Jess asked.

Kara sank onto a chair and closed her eyes. "Yes. It's bad."

"Oh, I'm sorry," Molly said. "Why—never mind. We shouldn't pry."

"The longer he goes without his first shift, the more dangerous it is. If he shifts for the first time when he's . . . when he's too big . . ." Tears burned in Kara's eyes. She couldn't say the rest. If he didn't shift as a cub, an effortless, relatively painless change might be impossible later. He might only partially shift—and then stay that way. She'd only read horror stories, so she didn't know, but the images in old books she'd seen as a child (thanks to her mother) haunted her sleep.

Kara jumped to her feet. "I'm sorry, you must think I'm crazy. I didn't get enough sleep last night, and I spent most of the day at the hospital with Jamie's nanny. She's an older lady and a good friend. I've been worried about her."

"You don't have to apologize!" Molly jumped up and came over to her with her arms wide. To Kara's surprise, she threw them around Kara and squeezed. "We're so glad we could help in our little way. Jamie is so cute. Both of us are rubbing our ovaries with this urge to have babies tomorrow because he's so cute."

"Rubbing ovaries isn't how you make a baby," Jess said. "I would've thought you and Edward had figured that out already."

All three women, even Kara, burst out laughing.

"Jess is getting ready for med school," Molly said, wiping her eyes. "It makes her think she knows everything."

Kara went over to Jamie, who had lost interest in the TV when the tiger story had turned to politics, and picked him up for another hug before she went back to work.

"Daddy!" he cried.

This time, he wasn't pointing at the TV.

The nearly white corn silk hair, so like his own as a child was similar enough, but as the tiny tot in front of him turned and beamed at Lars, the dimpled chin was the dead giveaway.

It was like looking at a picture of himself as a toddler.

But in real life.

As his eyes locked with the lad and his mini me stumbled toward him, Lars inhaled sharply.

Blue.

Ice-blue eyes.

The shape was different, curved more like Kara's, and as the little boy changed direction and walked over to Kara, burying his face in her lap and giving Lars a few shy peeks, he saw the profile.

My son.

There was no doubt. No need for tests.

Emotion pooled in his throat, making his tongue drop in the back of his mouth, his breath halting.

"Lars!" Kara's cry was an apology, the single word filled with longing and regret, pride and love, as she scooped the child into her arms and brought him closer.

"Daddy," the little boy said, soft and open, a sweet smile on his face.

"This is Jamie," Kara said, looking at the boy, who reached for Lars' nose with stubby, fat baby fingers that smelled like sugar and love.

The second he made contact, Kara began shouting, a high-pitched shriek that made no sense as skin became fur, fingers turned to claws, the little boy's clothing ripped, and Lars found himself precariously rocking on his heels with thirty pounds of tiger cub in his arms, face being licked by a wet, rough stretch of pink sandpaper, four paws and a tail spread over his torso.

"Jamie," Lars said, laughing as he hugged his cub, who wriggled out of his arms and scampered over to two women he struggled to remember. "Jamie."

"Oh my God!" the brown-haired one called out. "Molly! He's a tiger!"

Jess. That's right. Derry Stanton's fiancée.

"Kara said he was one!" Molly shouted back through laughter.

"Jamie?" Kara squeaked, tears streaming down her face, her neck twisting back and forth between Lars and the cub. "He's never—oh," she gasped, hand going to her throat, eyes wide. "This is the first time he's ever shifted."

Alarm flooded Lars's limbs, his mind spinning. "The first? Isn't that late? Is he okay? Is he healthy? Does he need a shifter doctor—"

"He's fine," she said, smiling sadly at Lars. "He's fine *now*. Lars, I am so, so sorry. I should have told you. I should never have kept him from you."

A loud racket behind a chair made them both look. Jamie's tiger face was digging through Molly's open purse, a lipstick rolling across the floor, a bag of gummi bears being shredded by their cub.

"I wonder if this is what Edward was like as a cub," Molly mused, arms wrapped around her midsection as she brayed with amusement. "Oh, and hi there, Lars," she added with an amused smile.

Molly Sloan. Lars had danced with her at the Stanton ranch recently. She was the center of so much controversy in the shifter world and also one of many women he'd once propositioned, however lightly. Her presence barely registered, though, as he processed the moment. All of that was in the past, as if life had been cut in half by the sharp line of Before and After.

His son. His *son* was here. His real life began *now*.

Lars took it all in, his breath coming in fits and gasps as he gave Jamie a tender look. The little cub looked up, a green piece of candy stuck to his wet, black nose. Widening his eyes, the glittering pupils narrowed.

And just as quickly as he'd shifted, little Jamie changed back to human, paws turned to fat fists that rooted around for candy. His naked little toddler back faced them all.

"Oh, my goodness!" Kara exclaimed, grabbing the boy and hiding him with her body, curled around him protectively as if she wanted to hold on to him forever. "Oh!" She was rattled, Lars could plainly see, tears streaking her makeup, an unfocused stare revealing an overwrought heart.

"Kara," he said softly.

"I'm so sorry!" she choked out, eyes wild, her body radiating shame. "I just—your mother. I was so afraid. So afraid she'd take the baby away. You—Your family has money and power and all I had . . . all I had was him." Smoothing the child's hair away from his face, she kissed the crown of his head.

"Again! Again!" Jamie shouted.

Kara kissed the boy again, but Lars knew that wasn't what he wanted.

Jamie wanted to shift again. To be in his tiger form, wild and loose, able to roam and explore. At that age, it was fun, nothing but pure joy, a visceral pleasure that was simple play in animal form.

A stab of envy coursed through him.

He remembered being so carefree.

Jess approached Kara with a sweatshirt, which she put on the boy. It was far too big for him, and he giggled, reaching for Lars.

"Daddy! Again!"

Kara flinched at the word "Daddy."

Lars smiled.

"Come here, son," he said, his voice cracking with emotion on the last word as Kara handed Jamie to him. Heart bursting with everything he'd assumed he would never feel, he embraced the wiggling child, feeling his heartbeat sync like gears in a newly oiled machine, finding the just-right fit.

A warm hand on his shoulder, accompanied by Kara's scent, made him feel complete.

"Want Nana! Want Nana!" Jamie began to chant, pushing off Lars' chest.

"Nana?" he asked, confused.

"His nanny. Our—Well, it's complicated. She's in the hospital right now. That's why I had to bring Jamie to work with me."

"Had to? Why?"

"Because I have to work, Lars. I have to support him. Us. Nana watches him while I work, but her heart—We thought she had a heart event, but it seems to be dehydration . . ."

Stone-cold certainty snapped him out of the strange, over-whelmed fog he found himself in.

"I wish I'd known," he said, taking her hand, gentle and tender.

"I'm so sorry. I'm a terrible person for keeping you from him. I just—I was so afraid you'd take him."

Lars pulled her into his arms, a surge of desire and comfort, of the future and the past, all blending inside him. Molly and Jess gave them understanding looks as they kept little Jamie occupied, flipping the television channel to cartoons. A small laugh escaped him, then a bigger one, the sound finally settling in his body as Kara relaxed slightly in his arms.

"I'll have someone check on her," he said. "One of my best people. He'll make sure she's getting the best care and report back to us if anything changes."

"Thank you, but—"

"Let me do this," he said. "Please. This is one time when vast, unlimited wealth comes in handy. She will have the best care, you understand?"

She smiled. "Thank you."

"You're right, though, Kara."

"About what?"

"I am going to take him."

The shove, he had to admit, was fair. Her arms pushed hard against him, but he stood steady, gripping her elbows.

"No! How dare you! No, no, you can't take Jamie from me—"

"I'm taking him. And you."

"And—what?"

"And your nanny. Anyone else in your life I need to know about?"

"What are you talking about, Lars?"

He swept his arm out as if gesturing to include the entire planet. "I'm taking you, Jamie, and your nanny to my home. You're officially done here at the Plat. You're coming home with me. That rat trap you live in is no more."

Her eyes narrowed as she stood at arm's distance. "What?"

"You heard me. I won't have my son living in that disgusting hellhole."

"That hellhole is a perfectly decent apartment!"

He just stared her down.

"Okay, but no—no—I don't want your money." Her mouth set with firm determination. "You accused me of being a gold digger. I won't let you turn me into that."

He had only one answer for that statement.

A kiss.

Eleven

K ara knew she'd been saying something, had been worried about something, had decided something, but now . . . Now . . .

Lars' kiss washed it all away. There was only the hot pressure of his mouth and luxurious pleasure sliding over her, through her, into her. His tongue probed the seam of her lips, separating them, and then he pushed inside her mouth to explore. As their tongues tangled, his fingers gently stroked her jaw, then cupped her face and tilted her to one side. Now they fit together like yin and yang, two pieces of a puzzle that had gone through life undone, lost, incomplete.

They were together. They belonged here. Her heart thrummed in steady agreement.

Mine, she thought. He's *mine*. And I'm his.

He pulled away and dropped featherlight kisses from her cheekbone to her temple. "Mine," he whispered into her ear, making her shiver. "My Kara."

Her name on his lips sent shivers through her body. The way he said it . . . nobody had ever said her name like that before, and yet it was as familiar as her own pulse.

What had they been arguing about? Oh, right. The apartment.

Money. Living together.

He turned her face in his hands and captured her mouth in another kiss, this one more fierce than the last. The whiskers on his jaw scraped across her chin, and blinding, burning sensation shot through her.

To hell with the apartment. It wasn't the hellhole he made it out to be, but it wasn't like she wouldn't be happy living with a fabulously rich rock star weretiger instead. And if she ever doubted her choice, she'd remind herself she'd done it for Jamie.

Because she was self-sacrificing like that.

Straining against him, she broke the kiss to drag her tongue along the whiskers and the dimple that was such a turn-on. He tasted better than cream. Smelled better than—

"Darling." His rough voice wouldn't have stopped her, but the strong thumb he planted over her lips did. "We . . . We're not alone."

"Don't mind us," Jess said cheerfully.

"No, we'll go into the other room," Molly said.

"We will?" Jess snorted. "Do you mean the closet?"

"There's a dressing room," Molly muttered. "We can—"

By now Kara had broken enough of the spell to bring her tongue back into her mouth, remove her hand from Lars' ass, and turn her face, only slightly, away from his. She couldn't bear to lose too much contact, so she intertwined her fingers through his.

Her thoughts were as scrambled as her feelings. Flushing with embarrassment, she couldn't bring herself to make eye contact with the two women at first. "Sorry, we shouldn't—I don't know what came over us. We should go—" Reality set in. She did have to go. She'd promised to work at least another hour. Carl must be going nuts. "Oh God. I have to get back to work. Lars, please—"

Before she could ask him to wait for her—again, but this time for just another hour or two—she saw Jamie.

He was deep asleep in Molly's arms, as limp as a noodle. His blond head was tilted back, resting against the curve of Molly's shoulder, and his mouth gaped open, his little pink tongue visible past the rounded, human baby teeth. Pale eyelashes fanned against his pink cheeks, their baby, peach-skin softness so unlike the tiger cub he'd been a moment ago.

Her baby had never looked so beautiful. She sank against Lars and felt joy rise up in her chest. The pounding of the Beat was deafening.

"You don't have to go back to work," Lars said firmly.

Such the alpha. As much as she'd love to give in to him and make love on Molly's sofa, reality be damned, they still had responsibilities. At least she did.

"I promised Eva," Kara said. She gave Lars a playful smile. "It's only another hour or two."

Jess jumped to her feet, propping the stuffed tiger on Jamie's tummy. "Forget that. I'd love to finish your shift for you."

"You can't do that," Kara said. "You're engaged to Derry Stanton. He'd never—"

"Never allow it?" Jess laughed. "I don't let him call all the shots, are you kidding? He'd be impossible if I didn't remind him what century we're living in now and then."

"And I'm happy to sit here with Jamie as long as you need," Molly said, beaming at Jamie in her arms. "He feels like heaven. So, so sweet. What an angel."

Lars chuckled. "Now that he's asleep, you mean. The first shift is notoriously exhausting. It's common for a child to sleep an entire day to recover," he said. "If he's anything like me, he'll be a devil as soon as he wakes."

"He's a *lot* like you," Kara said softly.

He squeezed her hand, caressing her knuckles with his thumb. Again the Beat thundered in her soul.

Jess patted each of them on the back as she strode to the door. "I'll explain to Eva on my way. It'll be fun to serve drinks again for a little while."

Kara tried arguing one more time. "No, I can't let you—"

"Yes, you can," Lars said.

"Imagine how jealous Derry will be when he sees me serving men at the club. He'll be a tiger in bed tonight!" Jess waved as she walked out the doorway. "So to speak!" Her voice trailed away with her laughter.

"Go on, you two," Molly said. "You need to, uh, talk. I'll be right here with your cutie. Come back after you've, um . . . talked." And then the damn woman *winked*.

He remembered Edward Stanton's incredible possessiveness toward Molly at the Stanton ranch during the emergency meeting of shifters. Now he understood.

"Thank you, Molly," he said with a grateful smile. Lars released Kara for a moment to stride over and stroke the dimple on Jamie's chin. "It has been a pleasure. A great pleasure."

"Yes, thank you so much, Molly," Kara said.

After another moment gazing at his son, Lars turned abruptly and hooked an arm around Kara's waist, grinning. "We need to, uh, talk," he said in her ear.

"But where?" Kara asked, waving goodbye to Molly. But Molly was staring at Jamie, completely oblivious to anyone else. Somebody had baby fever.

"I'll show you." Lars escorted her out of the boutique to the elevator. "This building has a lot of secrets." He kissed her on the mouth, lingering over her lips as they waited for the elevator to come. "Like you."

The Beat continued to chime in her head and chest, giving each step they took the feel of a dance, not unlike their first evening together. His hand felt warm and steady in hers, leading her through the building to the elevator and then down to the lobby, the same spot she'd been so shocked to see him only a few days earlier. How could so much change so quickly? Again, like their first meeting, they weren't entirely in charge of their own lives or each other. The current of fate had swept them up and taken them away to another world—thankfully together. She could look at his profile and see her future, all the days to come she would be with him, at his side, loving him.

I love you, she said silently, barely registering how he'd taken them to the service elevator behind the lobby reception desk.

He turned his profile to her and pinned her with his shining blue gaze. "I love you too," he said, sliding his hand up to her cheek.

"Can you hear me?" she whispered.

"In my heart," he said, then smiled. "I think. I'm not quite sure. But yes, I can hear you."

"Do you think we're going crazy?"

"If this is crazy," he said, "let's be crazy."

"That sounds like it's from one of your band's songs," she said with a laugh.

"I wrote it after I met you," he replied seriously.

They stepped onto the old elevator together, Lars put his palm over a large metal plate, and the car lurched downward. He pulled his phone out of his pocket and sent a quick text.

"Are we going to the wine cellar again?" she asked, not entirely eager to revisit that hard, cold table.

"It's time you saw the Novo Club."

"The what?"

"The club for shifters. Much more exclusive than the Platinum, although the ownership is interconnected."

"Lars, I'm not really part of that world. I'm not sure that's what I want to face tonight, meeting all the . . ." She didn't know how to put it. The elite? The rich snobs who'd excluded her all her life?

"You don't have to meet anyone. I've sent a message ahead for Morgan to escort us immediately to a private suite."

"Morgan?"

"Old man who runs the place. The butler. We can trust him."

They stepped out of the elevator into a room filled with leather chairs, bookcases, and well-polished antique tables, where an old man with white hair greeted them with a decanter, bottles of beer, and glasses on a silver tray.

"This way, Mr. Jensen," Morgan said. "And Miss Jablonski. I've started a fire in the Burgundy Room, and there are a few other refreshments." He turned and gestured for them to follow him through a narrow oak door that was black with age.

They walked down a dark hallway flickering with warm candlelight from wall sconces and then through another oak door, where Morgan stepped aside and bowed.

"Ring the bell if you need anything," he said, closing the door between them.

Kara didn't even turn around before Lars' hard body was pressing her against the heavy oak door.

"Kara," he growled into her hair, catching up handfuls of it in his fist as he kissed her neck, fierce and openmouthed, his teeth scraping her skin.

Desire flared in her as if there'd been no delay between the kiss upstairs, the wild lovemaking the other night, and their first passionate meeting. There was never anything but this, the two of them together. United. Loving.

One of his hands slid over her ribs and captured her breast through the fabric while his mouth continued to feast on her neck. Pleasure shot through her, turning her boneless. She clung to the door and let herself enjoy the sensations buffeting her body. This time she wouldn't feel guilty, embarrassed, or ashamed. This time she knew it was meant to be.

This time she was going to enjoy every second.

She went limp against the door and let herself sink into semi-consciousness. There were only his hands, his mouth, and the sensual spell he was casting over her body. His clever hands removed her clothes, and she felt a whisper of cool air against her bare skin, making her shiver.

"We need to warm you up," he said, holding her wrists with one of his hands over her head against the door. One broad palm rested in the small of her back, holding her in place as he licked and nibbled across her shoulders. She shivered again, this time from helpless pleasure. Her nipples, pressed against the hard door, tightened with need.

"Touch me," she said.

"Aren't I touching you?"

She arched under him. "Please—Lars—"

"Perhaps you should be more specific." He moved his hand down over the swell of her bottom and dug his fingers into her flesh. "God, you're so damn sexy," he growled, pushing his hips against her. Although he still wore his pants, he felt harder than she'd thought possible.

She turned her head and tried to twist around. She wanted to hold him and make him touch her where she was wet and tight for him. The pressure of him on her backside made her want it all inside her, now, immediately, to the hilt. "I want to touch you," she gasped.

Although he released her hands, he didn't move his body, which still pinned her to the door. He caressed her back and waist as if every inch needed to be touched slowly and carefully. The fabric of his shirt and wool trousers was rough against her bare skin, which only aroused her further. She was utterly vulnerable to him.

But not afraid. Not anymore. He was strong, but she had power over him as well. They were two halves of One, in complete balance.

This night would be the beginning of forever.

Another shiver racked her body as she felt the truth of it. They would have many days and nights together, but this moment was the beginning of their true bonding.

"Forgive me," Lars said, wrapping his arms around her shaking form and pulling her to face him. "I'm a selfish oaf. While I worship your body, you freeze to death."

She reached up and seized the first button on his shirt. "I'm not cold. I'm"—she worked the first one apart, then the next two—"excited." There. No undershirt, just him. She brushed her erect nipples against his golden chest hair and moaned, shameless.

"God, Kara, what you do to me." He kissed her hard but quickly on the mouth and then kicked off his shoes, attacked his belt, the fastener underneath, the zipper. In less than a second, the fine wool pooled at his ankles and he stood there in a pair of tight black boxers, his arousal as obvious as the love in his eyes.

With a grin, he gestured to a stately four-poster bed near a fireplace. Heavy tapestries lined the walls, and velvet drapes hung at each corner of the bed.

She didn't have time to notice anything else because Lars caught her up in his arms and flung her onto the mattress, a feat no mere human could've managed. As she gasped for breath, laughing, he jumped on the bed next to her. He was kneeling, hands on his hips, his blue eyes gleaming like burning embers in the firelight. He'd torn off the boxers, she noticed with approval, and then kept on noticing. Their other times together had been so rushed, she hadn't gotten a good look.

Or touch. She reached out, wrapped her fingers around him, and began massaging her thumb into the spot she hoped would—

Ah, yes. She'd found a good spot. He threw his head back, eyes closed, and began taking shallow breaths.

"You're beautiful too," she said, getting up on her knees for a better angle to stroke him. She kissed his throat, flicking her tongue over the tendons, the sweat, the racing pulse that so perfectly matched her own. While she continued squeezing his cock, she bit down lightly on the muscles leading to his shoulder, unable to resist his taste, which was salty, male, unique. She knew he would taste the same as a tiger, that this essence had nothing to do with their superficial form. If he were surrounded by a hundred other tigers, she could find him by scent alone. Instantly. And he could do the same with her.

His hand came down over her wrist, stilling her. "Enough," he said, his voice tight. "Take pity."

She smiled into his chest and inhaled more of his delicious scent. "I'm taking as much as I can." With a sigh, she tilted her head back and met his hot gaze.

"Kara," he said.

"Lars."

He caught her up in his arms and dropped his mouth to hers. Their tongues tangled in a hot, rushed dance. They angled their faces to deepen the kiss, feast on each other. His hands caught her shoulders and guided her onto her back as he climbed on top of her, graceful and confident, a predator with his prey.

Dangerous herself, Kara grabbed him by the back of the neck, her nails digging into his flesh, and pulled him down to her to continue the kiss. His knee knocked hers apart, spreading her thighs wide beneath him on the soft sheets. Arching, she reached for his cock and guided it between her legs, stroking it like she'd done a moment earlier, but harder, pulling him with long strokes to draw him inside her.

He took over then, palming her wetness, then rubbing her clit, sliding the tip of his cock around the entrance of her wet folds but not pushing deeper.

Teasing her.

"Now," she begged.

"Hm," he said, continuing to slide his thumb over her folds, circling her clit in lazy, unhurried strokes.

"I'll come when—Just do it," she said.

"What's the hurry?"

The pressure built inside her, making speech impossible. Her breath was coming in little bursts, not enough to fill her lungs. She was empty everywhere. "I want you inside me," she gasped. "Now. Now. Please."

"Hm," he said again, leaning down and licking the side of her face. Oh God. How did he know she loved that? And then he was kissing her breasts, lightly biting the hard nipples, his hot breath and sharp teeth sending electric shocks through every nerve in her body.

Just as she began to come, he grabbed her hips and thrust into her with a roar.

The old legends whispered to him as he pulled back, then entered her again as if one flesh, the sound of ancient voices carrying him forward, blending with The Beat. It overpowered him, turning him half-crazy as Kara's legs opened for him, her mouth on his, hot tongue running along the edge of his teeth, fingernails scratching his back, urging him deeper, welcoming him into her as if they could heal the rift of time.

His.

She was *his*, the fruit of their first coupling sleeping a few rooms away, his entire existence forever changed in less than twenty-four hours after coincidence turned into fate.

Twice.

A ready-made family was here now, his child sweet and perfect, a son to carry on the Jensen name. As he kissed Kara, his heart swelled, the brush of his chest against hers a delight as he moved in and out like the tick of a great clock, counting their love. Stroke by stroke, thrust by thrust, gasp by gasp.

How could it be so easy? Perhaps, he thought as she broke away and arched up into him, it was meant to be so simple.

For nearly three years he'd been unable to forget her.

Fate made him understand now.

"Lars," she said, his name stretched beyond sound, her sultry voice going tight and low at the end as emotion took over her flesh. Round, sensual breasts crushed against his ribs as he pushed his way home, again and again and again, her tight pussy so perfect it drowned out the world, the flow of soft curve against hard muscle making them merge into one.

The One.

He reached between them, fingers seeking her clit, the slick heat between her legs making him smile against her mouth. She gasped, then moaned against his lips, coming in seconds, bucking against his hand.

Restraint was never his strong suit. As she took the pleasure he so freely gave, he wrapped his free hand in her thick hair, the movement releasing a whiff of her perfume, and as Lars stared deep into Kara's eyes, he watched her unravel under him, body quaking as he moved inside her, stroking her in rhythm until she pulled him deep within.

The press of his open palm against her bare ass cheek, the feel of her hand on his shoulders, all the sensations mixed with his fiery need, lubricated by sweat and time and desire, turning their climax into something both finite and infinite, an apology and a celebration.

A vow and a homecoming.

He burst inside her, letting out a long groan of satisfaction as she took and took and took until she lost her voice, hoarse from crying out, completely disheveled from their primitive, atavistic lovemaking.

"I love you," he crooned in her ear, licking the vulnerable spot beneath her lobe. "I love you and the boy. I am so sorry you ever doubted me."

Kara began to cry, great fat tears pregnant with promise. "I'm the one who owes you an apology."

"You gave me the greatest gift anyone could give me, Kara.

A son. A healthy, well-loved son."

"Oh!" she gasped, smiling through her contrite expression, her face changing. Kara traced his brow, running her fingers along the bones of his eyes, down his cheek, ending at the chin dimple he had clearly passed on to Jamie. "Thank you."

He knew what she meant. "You've protected him. Enveloped him with unconditional love. It shows."

Tears began to stain the bedsheets, the dark spots growing larger as Kara cried without sound. "Yes. It's been my greatest mission in life."

"Mission accomplished. But now it's my turn."

"Your turn?"

"To make sure you both have unconditional love from me. And that you never, ever have to worry about anything again. Not money, not a place to live, not time. I want you to raise my children with me, Kara. Together."

"Child—*ren*?" she asked, the second syllable a squeak.

"In time, yes. In time." He rolled off her, and she snuggled against him, trusting and warm. As it should be.

"This is a lot. So fast. So soon."

"Is it?" He stroked her hair, loving the feel of it as it spilled over his bare chest. "It doesn't feel sudden. It feels like we've lost too many years. Time is the only resource I cannot give to you and Jamie in abundance. Everything else is nearly infinite."

"You forgive me?" she asked in a small, shy voice. "I really thought your mother would take him from me."

"Shhhh. What's done is done. What matters now is our future, together. Will you let me take care of you? I owe it to you."

"Owe?" She sat up in alarm. "You don't owe me anything. I'm not here for money or—"

"I owe you a deep debt, Kara."

"What?"

"Of gratitude. It's my turn to take care of Jamie. And you. And Nana. Let me pay you that debt."

"That's not how this works," she said with a choked laugh.

"If I simply said I wanted to lavish you and our son with all the riches of the world, would you accept?"

"No."

"Then let me do it as a thank-you for your good parenting. It's time for you to rest. To relax. To be nothing but my One and Jamie's mother."

"Your One?"

He took her hand and put it over his heart.

And then, without saying a word, he closed his eyes.

You can hear me? He asked without using his words.

Yes, she replied, clear as a bell.

We're together, he continued. *Your Beat is mine. Your love is mine. And my love is yours. All yours.*

Our love, she replied.

He kissed her then, a long, slow ritual of promise and fate.

And then he stood, walking across the room naked, reaching for the drawers full of clothes.

"Speaking of our love," he said to her as she stood and joined him, "let's get dressed and find Jamie."

"He's sleeping," she said, puzzled. "Jess and Molly told us they'd come if he wakes. That we could," she added with a giggle, "*talk*, then come and find him with them."

"I know," Lars said, love overflowing inside him. "But I want to look at him. See him. Watch him sleep."

Kara's arms encircled his waist as she pulled him into an

embrace. "I completely understand," she whispered.

He threaded his fingers in hers and squeezed, pulling her toward the door.

"Let's go."

Epilogue

One Year Later

The Mediterranean was stunning, but nothing could compete with Lars' eyes. Kara turned her camera away from the famously beautiful sea to snap yet another picture of her husband. He reclined next to her on the beach, wearing only a pair of white swim shorts that set off his tanned skin, his muscled physique, and those gorgeous blue eyes. By now she had quite a portfolio of photographs of him—in Greece, Boston, Tuscany, Tokyo, California, Patagonia, Belize . . . They'd traveled the world, learning about each other, intertwining their lives, deepening their love.

She adjusted her hat, an enormous white floppy thing Lars had bought her at a market in Athens, and stretched out her legs into the white sand. One year ago today, they'd come to this private Greek island for their honeymoon. Now they were celebrating their first anniversary and—

Well, he didn't know about that yet.

Like last year, Nana stayed with Jamie in their new Boston penthouse and video chatted with them several times a day. A year ago, Jamie had been new to his tiger form and shifted constantly, usually for their calls. These days, however, as a big three year old, he only shifted when he was in trouble and wanted to hide.

Today Kara was the one hiding something. She'd buried a small present inside the picnic blanket, and she was trying to decide when to share it with him. After they ate the fabulous Greek cuisine packed for them at the five-star restaurant or before? He was about to uncork the wine, and he might notice—

The hot sun felt so good, but it was making her thirsty. She opened the picnic basket, checked on her hidden package at the bottom, and took out a bottle of chilled mineral water.

"Got you," he said, setting aside his own phone.

She laughed and wiped her lips. "I told you, please don't take pictures of me without warning me first! You always catch me at the most unflattering moment."

"There is no such thing," he said. "You are always beautiful. Always."

"Just wait until you see—" Even he couldn't think she was beautiful when she was puking her guts out. Oh Lord, she was so bad at keeping a secret. She had to tell him now.

"Lars?"

"Kara, my love?" Smiling, he reached into the picnic basket.

She lurched forward and grabbed his arm. "Wait!"

His eyebrow arched. "Can't keep your hands off me, can you darling?" He caught her wrist and pulled her across the blanket into his lap. Strong, curious hands slid under the flimsy bottom of her swimsuit. His fingers began caressing, exploring.

"Mm," she said, forgetting everything except the feel of his hands. She nuzzled his neck, dropping kisses along his throat, not minding the sand that stuck to her tongue. Because the island was private, they were able to shift and roam together, a wonderful treat after the past month in Boston, but she would always prefer being together like this. In their human form they could talk, laugh, and sing together; they could go to the park with Jamie; they could take pictures and sail and snorkel; they could make love.

Several times a day, on occasion.

Like now . . . So many advantages to a private beach . . .

"You were saying something?" he asked. He'd been nibbling on her left nipple through the stretchy fabric of her bikini, teasing it to a hard point.

She could only moan.

"Kara?" He lifted his head and fixed those blue eyes on her. "You wanted to talk."

"I did?"

He stroked her belly, occasionally dipping between her legs for a quick stroke. "I think you did."

"I don't remember."

"It could be sunstroke. Perhaps we should get you inside where it's cool and you can recover." He crawled down her body and buried his face between her legs—just for a second—and then sat up on his heels. He stroked the bottom of her foot, tickling her. "You do look a little flushed."

She giggled and sat up. "It's not sunstroke."

"If you're sure." He bent over and sucked her toes into his mouth.

Oh God. She melted into the sensation for a second—perhaps a little longer—before making herself draw her feet back. "Hold it, you're right. I have something to tell you."

"Nana's in love," he said. "He's a little younger than she is, but I don't think she minds."

Kara laughed. It was true. Nana had been dating a shifter

from the Novo Club now for two months. Kara had never seen her so happy. Talk about a heart condition. She was as giddy as a teenager with her first crush.

"No, that's not what I wanted to talk about," she said. "This is about us."

"You're finally going to confess to dressing up as Beauty and seducing this handsome guy at a charity ball a few years ago."

"No, that's not it either."

"Because he was devastated when you disappeared," he said. "Completely fell apart. He was utterly useless without you."

Her heart pounded along with the Beat in her chest. *I love you*, she said silently.

I love you too, he replied.

She'd lost the taste for teasing him about her secret. Now she just wanted to tell him as soon as possible. Brushing the hair off his forehead, she kissed him quickly and then reached into the picnic basket. She drew out the small package and handed it to him.

He frowned as he took it from her. "I thought you were going to tell me something, not give me a gift. I have yours back at the cottage."

"Open it," she said.

"But—"

"Open it." She tapped the cloth wrapping. "Please?"

He shrugged, sat up, and unfolded the fabric surrounding the soft little object she'd bought as soon as she was sure.

A stuffed tiger.

Eyes wide, he looked up at her. "Does this mean . . ."

"Does it mean what?"

"I don't think Jamie would be interested in a new stuffed tiger, so . . ."

"Yes?" She clasped her hands together, her breath coming faster. Was he happy? She'd assumed he would be, but it would make travel more awkward than it already was just with Jamie, and . . .

He caught her up in his arms and pinned her onto the blanket. "Oh, Kara, oh Kara," he said between kisses. He held her face and touched his nose to hers. "I've never been so happy."

She laughed. Thank God. "Me too."

"How do you feel?" He rolled off her, moving his weight to the sand. "Are you tired? Nauseated? Emotional?"

"Definitely emotional," she said, wiping away a tear. How could life be so good?

"As am I." He kissed her again, then sat up. "As it happens, I have something for you as well."

"I thought you said it was in the cottage," she said.

"This is just a little something. Not your anniversary present." He crawled over to his pants, folded next to the picnic basket, and took a small velvet box out of his shorts pocket.

"You already gave me a heck of a ring," she said, holding her hand out and wiggling her fingers. Talk about rocks. It was enough to make her become a geologist.

"Open it." He set it in her lap.

In the past year, she'd learned how extravagant he could be. She was almost afraid to find out—or underestimate—how much money he'd spent this time. She flashed him a loving smile and opened the box.

Resting there in the satin were four little gold tigers on a chain. Four.

"Hey!" She looked at him, struggling for words. "You *knew*?"

He grinned. "I think I knew before you did."

She smacked him on the shoulder. The tigers were beautiful,

very, very beautiful, but she had to hit him for putting her through that.

He only laughed and rolled onto his side next to her, hooking his arm around her waist and burying his face in her belly. "I can hear her."

Why had she doubted the bond they shared? "So can I," she said, stroking his hair.

"I can hear her Beat."

"It's getting noisy around here," Kara said.

He looked up at her, his blue eyes shining. "I love noise. Why do you think I became a rock star?"

The End

Loved Molly, Jess and Sophia? Read all about how they met their One . . . and watch for new books in the series!

Grab a sneak peek at *The Billionaire Shifter's True Alpha*, book 5 in the Billionaire Shifters Club series:

Sneak Peek at True Alpha

"Tea?"

Asher Stanton's casual inquiry made Zachary Hayden go cold. Zach knew that someone as powerful as the eldest Stanton didn't give a hoot about whether he was comfortable and certainly wasn't monitoring his needs.

Before Zach could reply, Stanton sighed, the man's strong face like a slab of polished stone with two glittering gemstones for eyes.

"Of course. You're American. How silly of me. Coffee?" An eyebrow rose along with his voice, the British clip thick and aristocratic, designed to shrivel balls. The eyes betrayed nothing.

Squaring his shoulders, Zach sat up taller. Broader. Bigger than before.

Before the lab accident.

Caffeine was the last substance he needed circulating through his bloodstream right now.

Well, *second* to last. Shifter serum took top prize in that category, but as Zach scratched his forearm absentmindedly, trying to buy himself time to answer Stanton's question, he bitterly recognized that the choice on *that* issue was long gone.

They'd just met for the first time, brutal handshakes administered, and now they waited for Zach's boss to appear so they could get on with business. Important business.

Life-altering business.

Asher cleared his throat, the sound a melodic growl filled with the implication that Zach was being rude by not answering his tea inquiry. Since The Incident, Zach's senses were keener, sharper, picking up on emotional vibrations and social cues the average human would never catch.

Zach was anything but *average* now.

And today Zach would be discharged from his extended stay at LupiNex. Asher Stanton was the final hurdle.

"Sure," he barked out, simply to end the tension, half hoping Asher would leave to acquire the drink, half hoping all these petty macho domination games would continue so Zach could see what his body did in the presence of a pack leader. *His* pack leader.

It was anyone's guess.

The door opened suddenly, too soon for Asher to have called a secretary. Both men turned to look. A woman's blue-cloth-covered leg crossed the wedge of space made by the open door, the click of a high heel on the office floor making Zach flinch, the sound triggering a reaction like aluminum foil on an amalgam filling.

Navy wool slacks, shined two-toned heels. A white lab jacket, so similar to the one he'd donned for the past decade between undergrad, graduate school, and work.

Flaming red curls hanging over one shoulder, her long ponytail coiffed with care.

"Dr. Baird," Asher said, standing suddenly. Formality was the man's idea of comfort, Zach realized, while Asher went through the motions as Dr. Samantha Baird joined the meeting. She'd been his boss for the past three years here at LupiNex, the first to recruit him for the shifter DNA project, an initiative so ludicrously fringe he'd had no choice but to join.

And a project that had sealed his fate in more ways than one.

"Mr. Stanton," she said, voice controlled but her cheeks pink, eyes bright. She turned to Zach and caught his eyes, her look softening. "Zach."

She reminded him of his grandmother, now long dead. The caring eyes.

"Your timing is impeccable," Asher said to her. "We require a coffee-and-tea tray for three. Cream and sugar."

Her face froze, still looking at Zach, mouth tightening, eyes going hard behind her glasses.

"Excuse me?" She didn't bother to look at Stanton as she asked the rhetorical question. The man was scowling at papers in a manila folder. Zach's gaze skittered to the folder's tab, where he found his name scrawled in black Sharpie.

Of course.

"Make certain you bring whatever beverage you prefer as well," Stanton said, not looking up. "While I shall endeavor to keep this meeting brief, we have much to discuss. Refreshments might help."

"I prefer nothing," Sam said smoothly, recovering step by step as she walked past Zach, lowering herself into a chair to his left. "I just had a latte." Her eyes narrowed as she glared at the top of Asher's head. "A double. I'm already quite refreshed, Mr. Stanton."

Stanton's nostrils flared. He gave no other indication of emotional reaction to her rejection of his patronizing assumption. Zach's body tensed, heat flushing his neck and upper chest, the feeling fleeting but disconcerting. As he inhaled slowly, he smelled it.

All of it.

Every bit of subtext in the room had an odor. Sam's anger, Asher's annoyance, Zach's own confusion. Sparks of sexual interest between Sam and Asher literally smelled like sulfur and wine and embarrassingly intimate pheromones, a rich, intoxicating scent that turned Zach into a voyeur.

Could you be a Peeping Tom with your nose? If yes, then Zach was guilty as hell.

"It's fine," he cut in, breathing through his mouth, arousal snaking its way across his skin, the scent a contagion. "By the time we're done, I'd planned to drink something stronger anyhow." His mouth curled up as Sam examined him, reading his body as much as she listened to his words. He knew before his conscious mind could form the thought that the desire blooming in him wasn't for her.

It just *was*.

"You're flushed," she said, reaching for his wrist. As her fingertips found his pulse, his hand burned. Regulating his temperature had been a problem since The Incident (as he thought of it), his blood running hot. Asher's eyes locked on the spot where Sam's fingers met Zach's skin.

Zach smelled his frown before he saw it.

"I'm fine," he protested, tearing his arm away from Sam, moving in his seat, leaning forward and pressing his elbows into his knees. His hand reached up to rub his freshly shaved chin.

"Shall we then? Given Dr. Baird's caffeinated state, this should be quick," Asher said, eyes on her fingers.

The ones that had just touched Zach.

"What's left to discuss? It's time for me to go home. Leave LupiNex. I appreciate all the care you've given me, and Mr. Stanton—Gavin, I mean—has been more than generous with the settlement regarding my, um . . ." Zach's rapid-fire speech died down as he tried to ignore Asher Stanton's withering look.

"The lab accident," Sam interjected. "The serum injection."

The Incident.

Asher held a sheet before him and began reading. "The subject," he read, eyes moving to glance at Zach, "injected less than two cc's from a syringe into the tip of his left index finger, plunging third-generation serum made from batch X31 into his body. Three witnesses were present. In less than a second, subject's eyes turned red. Within three seconds, subject's body developed fur. Approximately four seconds post-injection, subject's bone structure elongated, clothing shredding—"

"We've all read the reports, Mr. Stanton," Sam said. "No need to go over every gruesome detail."

"Gruesome." Zach repeated her word. "What an understatement." He gave Asher a wry smile. The man didn't react.

Zach continued. "I'll sum it up. Within seconds after accidentally injecting myself with a serum I wasn't given full information about, I turned into a wolf. According to eyewitnesses, I growled, howled, jumped through a plate glass window dividing a conference room from a hallway, and promptly froze. Within five seconds, my shift devolved, leaving me with seventeen broken bones, a torn meniscus, rearranged organs, a complete alteration in my bone structure and musculature, and enough reconstructive surgery over the past eight months to make me a candidate for the Witness Protection Program."

No one in the room laughed.

"I've healed. It's time to let me go." He'd used the same words three weeks ago, his tone a plea. This time, it was a demand.

"You left out the part describing the fact that you possess

shifter abilities, Zachary," Asher intoned.

"Don't call me that," he said sharply. "It's Zach." Zachary was what his parents had called him when they were alive. The asshole sitting across the desk didn't deserve to call him by his full name.

Asher didn't blink. "You possess powers no human has ever held. And your appearance is notably . . . changed." Pictures inside the folder in Asher's hands showed him *before*. Five feet nine, one hundred fifty pounds, a lab rat. Glasses and an old Michigan hoodie. Size nine men's shoe.

As he stretched his restless legs before him and reached up to scratch his chin, he could see the *after* in his body. Seven inches of new height. Seventy new pounds of solid muscle. Size thirteen shoe.

Everything had grown. He willed himself not to think about certain body parts, ones that twitched as his blood pumped fiercely through him, his nose catching the wafting scent of a woman's perfume from the nearby elevator. Electricity shot up the root of his cock, making his gut clench. Being watched twenty-four seven in a clinical setting for eight months wasn't doing him any favors sexually, either.

Sam's turn to cock an eyebrow. Zach could feel a lie in the air, as if Asher and Sam weren't quite telling him everything, but couldn't explain why.

"Look. It's not like I want to be a wolf. I just won't shift. It's simple," he declared, pinging his attention between Sam and Asher.

"If it were simple, we wouldn't be having this meeting. Your powers are considerably more complex than you realize," Asher replied.

"He's right," Sam added. "You can't just go back to your regular life."

Zach slid the rolled cuff of his white business shirt up to reveal scars that laced the long lines of his bones. "You think I'll just 'go back'?" He lifted a section of his wavy brown hair off his forehead, fingertips grazing the thick scarring there. "Do I need to show you the rest?" He resisted reaching for his belt buckle.

"No. We're well acquainted with all the damage to your body," Sam said in a pained voice.

Asher's eyes just narrowed.

"I can't 'go back' to a life that isn't mine anymore."

"Is this about money?" Asher asked drolly, a touch of cynicism obvious.

"It's about freedom."

The man's dismissive huff made the hair on Zach's neck stand up. "Mr. Hayden, I assure you, freedom is the very last priority you should have at this moment. Security is considerably more important."

"Fine to say when *you're* free. Tell me how important security is when you feel like a prisoner." Zach was on his feet, hands in fists, fury rising in his chest, a lump he couldn't swallow down. "I'm out of here."

Sam looked at Asher, the two communicating some thought that made Zach pause.

"The shifting is under control?" Asher asked her, his tone clear; there was only one acceptable answer.

"In a controlled environment, yes," she replied, clinical and dry.

"You haven't tested him out there? In the real world?"

"Mr. Stanton, how, exactly, do you suggest we 'test' Zach's shifter powers and ability to manage his shifting in the human world? There isn't an ethics board for this. Peer-reviewed studies don't exist. We're making this up as we go along."

Zach winced. Those last words were kryptonite to a scientist.

"He's healed?"

"Yes. All the damage from the initial incident has been addressed. His appearance is, ah . . . altered. As you can see."

Zach resisted the urge to flex a bicep. Turn green. Pick up a car. Roar.

"I'm leaving," he reiterated.

"Can you control yourself around women?" Asher asked, his voice as casual as if he were asking Zach's golf handicap.

Zach avoided Sam's eyes. "What?"

"My kind experiences uncontrolled shifting during two phases: puberty and . . . Well, the other one isn't important. Silly old legend." He smirked. "Can you control your shifting around women?"

"I haven't shifted since The Incident."

Asher looked shocked. "Not once?"

"No."

"Have you tried?"

"No."

"Could you shift if you wanted to?"

Zach's fingertips tingled, his toes spreading, thighs thickening as rage fueled the prodromal symptoms of a shift. A thick, earthy scent of a woman a few floors away fed into the deepening change in him, making linear thought difficult.

"Yes," he said in a voice darker than he'd intended.

"But you can control it?" Asher sounded skeptical.

"Of course," he and Sam replied in unison, though she gave him major side-eye.

A long, slow breath came out of Asher, his attention suddenly entirely devoted to Sam. "I defer to your professional opinion."

"I suspect you never defer," she shot back, "but it is a relief to know you view me as a professional."

"You created this mess with the serum. I have no choice but to trust you to solve the problems related to it."

"I'm not a problem," Zach retorted. A blur of colored smoke and ribbons, of music and sweet spun sugar danced on his skin, the scent of some unnamed woman like fast-growing morning glories wrapping around his cock. She was in the building somewhere, his body thick where it shouldn't be, his restraint thinning as he stood on the threshold of freedom.

Now? Of all times to pick up the scent of a woman he couldn't ignore, it had to be *now*?

"But you *are* a complication. If it were as simple as letting you go home, trust me, we would," Asher said, brow furrowed. He looked at Sam and waited, impassive.

Zach's heart slammed against his ribs, the beat matching sex thrusts, going faster and faster until he felt the fine beads of sweat under his collar, his armpits on fire, his lip soaking. He had to get out of here now.

He had to find *her*.

"Trust me," he said calmly, fighting to hide the struggle within. "Besides, if I'm wrong, I'll just come back." That was a lie. Every word out of his mouth was a lie, rushing out of him pell-mell, his urgent need to go and find *her* making him say whatever it took.

Asher blinked exactly once. "If you are wrong, humans could die. If you are wrong, you could reveal our kind. Our survival depends on your discretion, much to my chagrin. You've hardly proven yourself trustworthy."

Rage pumped Zach up, making him lean in, aggressive and dominant. "If anyone has anything to prove, it's *you*."

A flicker of emotion registered in Asher's face as he stood.

Sam touched Zach's arm, her voice low and soothing.

"I think we need to give Zach the benefit of the doubt. He still works here. Let him go home, Asher." Her use of Stanton's first name was touching. "He'll be back tomorrow for work. He's suffered enough. I can see his frustration."

Zach looked down at his crotch. Was it that obvious?

"We can acclimate him to his new reality," she insisted.

Zach's new reality was blurring around the edges as he smelled *her*, floors away, her hair tickling his nose, the need to bury himself in the unnamed woman such a primal craving that he couldn't stand being away from her for a minute longer. Crossing the small office, he grasped the doorknob and turned, looking only at Sam.

"I am one hundred percent in control of myself. I'll see you tomorrow."

Slamming the door on Asher Stanton's protests, Zach ate up the floor, strides long and determined as he bypassed the elevator and went straight for the stairs. A magnetic pull told him to go up, two stairs at a time until he reached the twelfth floor.

Barreling through the metal door, he tore down a hallway, pivoting until he stared at the sign.

The Platinum Club.

He'd been here once before, for a LupiNex holiday party, but memory served as no anchor, his body very much in the present, second by second, step by step, as her scent grew stronger. Loud, booming laughter filled his ears, the sound like church bells, like heaven, like every musical note forged into a single drumbeat meant for him.

"Excuse me. Can I help you?" A catlike woman wearing a dark pantsuit and gold hoop earrings gave him a smooth look, her face placid but authoritarian. Old enough to be his late mother but too sophisticated, she looked like she ran the place.

"I'm here for—" He halted, hearing the change in his voice.

No.

No.

He met her eyes, seeing a cold disapproval morph into disbelief as she reached into her jacket and pulled out a phone.

"Derry!" she called out, the word meaning nothing to Zach. Racing away from her, the unnamed woman's scent strengthening, he turned to the right of a large bar and found a beast of a man with a blonde human in his lap, the two drinking out of large wineglasses.

"Sorry, chap, the Plat's not open yet. We're—"

"Here's the sangria! Derry, get another glass."

Zach turned to find a goddess holding a pitcher, her long black hair like spun obsidian, her scent the answer to every mystery he'd ever pondered.

And just then he realized how terribly wrong he'd been moments ago.

Nothing was under control.

Least of all him.

Sophia Stanton would've recognized him even without the supernatural senses her bear shifter nature gave her. And right now every one of those senses—sight, hearing, smell, taste—was electric with the sudden charge of awareness. She registered his skin, his muscles, his blood, the wave of his hair, the tangy, tantalizing allure of his sweat.

She would've recognized him if he'd shrunk to a tenth of his original size, been dipped in blue paint, dressed as an elf, and stuck in a toy shop window with a price tag on his ear.

"You," she whispered.

Him, a voice inside her echoed.

The pitcher of sangria in her hands suddenly felt like a brick, a millstone, a lifetime.

His lips parted, but only a soft, deep growl came forth.

Heat flooded her as she recognized the new part of him. Not completely human anymore, this man, the one who had humiliated her so long ago, yet the one she couldn't forget.

No, she wouldn't even admit it to herself. He hadn't hurt her; he was simply a fool. An idiot. Too stupid to realize what a tremendous loss he'd suffered when he'd turned down her invitation last year. A real man—shifter or human—would've been honored. Real men begged for her attentions and thanked her profusely afterward, right before they begged for more.

Being a bear shifter, even a female bear shifter, she'd frequently indulged. Not as often as Derry—let's be serious, her twin brother had been pathological in his sexual escapades before he'd gotten engaged to Jess—but as often as she pleased, which was quite often.

She wasn't ashamed of who she was. Unlike her brother Gavin, who was always running from his nature, trying to control the wolf within, she reveled in who she was: a bear shifter with a passion for life. Not just sex, but adventure. Action. Achievement.

That night in the elevator, however, this man standing before her now with lust radiating from his eyes had turned her down as quickly and as forcefully as her previous lovers had begged for more.

But how things had changed. He didn't look as if he would reject her *now*.

My goodness. He was as flushed and eager as an adolescent shifter at his first orgy. His eyes were black as licorice, the golden brown shoved aggressively aside by some biochemical process in him, his sensual mouth moist from hungry swipes of his tongue. The man was bigger—taller even—with the thick build of a beast in command.

She could hear his accelerated pulse, the shallowness of his hot breath, and even the lurid thoughts in his brain—a mantra of words such as *kiss, lick, taste, pound, thrust, take.*

You.

"How lovely to see you again," she purred, savoring the way his eyes darkened further, the rush of his blood pumping through his veins, making the pulse on his neck jump.

She hadn't made an impression *then*, but she certainly was making one *now*.

Sophia held out her hand, eyes holding his, letting him know she saw his arousal, that she could manipulate it, that—this time, at last—he was her prisoner. "I don't believe I ever got your name. I'm Sophia Stanton."

He dragged his gaze away from her face to stare at her hand a moment before grabbing it between both of his and bringing it to his lips.

At the feel of his tongue against her knuckles, her amusement faltered, replaced by a blast of molten need.

Him.

If it weren't for years and years of practice, she would've melted to the floor in a puddle, speech impossible. But she did have practice managing her own desire, and she brought it to heel, with far more effort than was reasonable, by snatching her hand out of his grip. Heart thudding in her ears, she staggered back a step. "Your name?" she demanded, although her voice quivered.

He raised his head slightly, and his eyes met hers. Dark pools of hot pleasure she wanted to dive into naked and screaming the name she didn't know.

"Zach Hayden," he said, his voice rough. She heard a faint howl at the edges of his speech, the way a werewolf sounded when he was on the verge of a shift.

She studied him more closely, acknowledging he was not only more muscular now but taller, impossibly so. As a shifter, she was so accustomed to seeing incredible transformations in her friends and family, she hadn't paused to think why her brother's human employee, whom she'd fruitlessly propositioned once on a drunken whim ages ago, was now a sexually potent werewolf with claws straining at his fingertips.

Wait.

The accident at the lab. The human researcher. It must've been him.

And he was about to shift—here, now.

Belatedly she realized the danger. They were at the Platinum Club, not a shifter haven. This was no place for a man to turn into a wolf. She was here with Derry and Jess as the club opened, so thankfully the place had few patrons, but there were enough—plus the human workers who could not be exposed to an uncontrolled shifter.

Assuming that was what she saw unfolding before her.

"Derry!" Eva appeared, her typical smoothness pushed aside by concern. "Can you help with this—he's—this human? Shifter?"

"I've got him," Sophia declared.

"Are you sure?" Derry's voice was a curious mixture of concern and amusement.

"Since when have I ever had a problem managing your kind?"

"My kind?" he replied, the amusement taking over.

"Men in heat," she shot back.

"Take him downstairs!" Eva called out to her. "Morgan will be expecting you."

Shoving aside her questions for later, Sophia risked touching him again, clamping her hand around a muscled bicep that was tightening into a predator's foreleg, and hauling him with her to a service corridor behind the bar.

Even that slight contact, her fingers on his arm with thick fabric between, burned hot enough to make her flinch. Each step they took together was timed to her heartbeat, loud enough now to drown out the sounds of the bar's Friday night dance music blaring from the speakers overhead, the nightclub about to open.

The service elevator, thank God, was already on this floor, and she pushed him inside and joined him, breathless and confused. She set her palm on the metal plate that would bring them to safety downstairs.

To the secret Novo Club.

"Sophia."

His voice didn't make the usual path—it didn't travel through the air to her ears to her brain, where the nerves deciphered the sound and filed it away rationally. Instead, the sound of her name on his lips pierced her skin, sliced through flesh, muscle, and bone until it found her heart, where it embedded itself deep inside, barbed and deadly.

The chestnut waves of his hair were spreading into his cheeks, his eyes flashing golden over his narrowing jaw.

She slapped him. She was taller than most men, with the strength of a bear who lifted pianos for exercise, and her hand knocked him off-balance. "Control yourself!"

His animal features flickered, faded. Very human, very male eyes captured hers. A slow smile spread over his lips, and she shivered.

"I thought you didn't like men who controlled themselves," he said slowly, raising an eyebrow.

A memory struck her as powerfully as her hand had just hit his jaw: her hand sliding up his (then narrow) chest, pushing away the lapels of his lab coat to feel the beat of the heart that, for some reason, she'd wanted to touch.

"Come home with me," she'd said, mindlessly following the impulse to get him into her bed, gift him with her body.

But he'd refused her. The shock hadn't left her for days—if ever.

For he had been the only man to refuse her.

She put a hand on the wall of the elevator for support. Silently she begged the elevator to descend more quickly. To the Novo Club. To safety. Something was wrong with him. Something that could hurt her. Trained as a nurse, she wasn't too proud to admit there were times everyone—even she—needed assistance.

And as Zach's look intensified, every nerve ending in her body simultaneously stood on end, buzzing, the sound of thousands of vibrations all coming together to form a single beat.

One that drowned out all her fear and replaced it with something worse.

Fate.

Two

The world was a heartbeat.

And Zach was its heart.

As he watched the elevators close, he felt like four chambers of red, pounding flesh, beating in sync to pump himself into the world, taking it over, king of it all. Sophia's fear bubbled off her like hot water on a griddle, bouncing and tingling until it evaporated into nothing but the memory of the ripple. She was pure beauty in pulsing form, every single cell of her deliciously large frame filled with nothing but attention to him.

Just as nature intended.

Power coursed through him like a drug, making his head light with an irrepressible urge to smile, to laugh, to take in the wonder of his connection to, well, *everything*.

Everything but her.

Time to fix that. Now.

Drawn to Sophia, he reached for her shoulders, finding resistance that only spurred him on, his body moving as if choreographed, her hot, sweet mouth against his before he knew it. She was tall, impossibly so, but even more outrageous was the fact that he was taller. Last year she'd towered over him.

Last year he'd ached to say yes to her offer of a one-night

stand, but principle had left him lonely that night. Her reputation preceded her: Sophia Stanton, the wildly sex-positive billionaire heiress who bedded men the way most women shopped for shoes.

Now, though, their mouths fit perfectly together, tongues tangled as his hands, big and strong, plunged into her long hair, grasping close to her scalp with an intensity that made her gasp— and made him grin. Power was intoxicating, a thrill ride that made the kiss like a roller coaster, highs and lows a dizzying race, stomach fluttering, body braced for impact.

He knew exactly where he wanted to impact her, too.

"Zach," she moaned in that maddening British accent, the sound shooting straight to his cock, her silky dress nothing more than an obstacle in his hands, her thigh pressed against his aching erection like she was propping up his world. Her palms crawled up his broadening back, fingernails digging into the thick muscle he'd acquired. As his breath quickened, he devoured her mouth to the point of madness, hands finding luscious breasts with nipples like marbled diamonds, taut and ready to be licked by the thousand tongues that filled his mouth, all ready for her.

"Sophia." The syllables rolled off his tongue as he broke the kiss, but he couldn't bear the space between them, her expression dazed, cheeks flushed. With more force than he assumed she possessed, he found himself pulled back into a fevered kiss, her mouth demanding his full attention once more.

Dominance didn't come into play as they tangled together in a twisting tumble of flesh. Sophia gave back every ounce of force, matching him with a fervor that made him insane.

Made him need to rut. To breed. To spill himself into her.

To mount her like an animal and take as much as she gave.

And then take some more.

Nimble fingers moved against his shoulders, harsh and needy, as Sophia groaned deep in her throat, then tore away, leaving Zach openmouthed and chilled. Her eyes took him in, worried and alert, fingers going to her mouth in shock.

"You're shifting. Completely. We have seconds, if we're lucky!" she gasped.

The elevator's *ding* went ignored as fire shot through his blood, his ears perked and growing. Every sound intensified, his vision going sharp as he opened his eyes to find Sophia pushing him away, her hands flat against his chest, eyes bright, hair mussed.

"Morgan!" she cried out as Zach's vision made every feature of the elevator stand out, the edges of each metal panel like glow sticks. As he took a step out onto the floor, his shoe sole cracked against stone, the sound close to a thunderclap to his heightened senses, then stopped, his foot growing, the *ping! ping! ping!* of thick loafer stitches popping like Bubble Wrap.

The length of his forearm was nothing but fur, his bones aching with a maddening release that turned pain into unadulterated pleasure. Sophia's scent, a mix of soap and sweat and pussy, oh, *pussy,* made him lunge at her, catching her at an angle, her ass up against his front in a second, his cock ripping through the trouser seams as he morphed and grew, blood racing where he needed it most, jaw stretching to accommodate more kisses.

More *teeth.*

He arched against her ass as the shreds of his clothing pooled in strips of forgotten civility, his hands peeling her dress up, her ass moving in rhythm with his thrusts. So close, so close, so—

The needle that struck his hindquarters from behind was a gnat, a mosquito bite, a pinprick, but the tiny reservoir of humanity left in him knew what it was before the tip withdrew. He turned to find Sam and Asher Stanton behind him, Asher's face twisted with bitter cynicism.

The last words he heard before he hit the floor came from a deep baritone dripping with contempt and, Zach swore, a slight laugh.

"One hundred percent control?"

And with that, the world went dark.

———

Sophia was too stunned to respond right away. Hand planted on the wall for support—Zach had almost knocked her over—she struggled to regain her composure. It wasn't simply shock from *his* loss of control, from his sudden dangerous shift, or even the way he'd grabbed and kissed her.

It was her own loss of control. If they hadn't been in the elevator, if they hadn't reached the Novo—their private shifter club—if they hadn't been surrounded by others . . .

Would she have stopped him?

The absurdity of it struck her out of her daze. Of course she would've stopped him. He'd morphed involuntarily into the lust-driven, half-animal state typical of pubescent shifter males who were learning the scope of their powers.

"Does he live?" Asher asked, sneering down his long nose at Zach's prone, half-naked body, now human, on the floor.

The LupiNex researcher, Dr. Samantha Baird, was already kneeling at Zach's side. Sophia had met her last winter when a powerful serum made from modified shifter DNA had been stolen from the lab, endangering the safety and secrecy of their world.

Sam pressed a hand to his throat, then his heart. "Yes," she said, nodding in relief. "He's breathing. Strong pulse. Merely unconscious."

"Unfortunate," Asher said, each syllable cold and clipped.

Sam looked up in outrage. "How can you say that? This man almost died working for your family. And now he has been sedated by an elephant tranquilizer."

"That . . . *man* . . . asked for death when he touched my sister," Asher said.

Anger drove Sophia to shake off the last of her shock. She straightened to her full height and planted herself in front of her eldest sibling, who was so often confused about his place in her life. "If my *brothers* insisted on murdering every man who touched me, the bloodshed would land each one of them in prison. And deservedly so." She glared at him, holding his gaze. "And trust me, Asher. You don't want to know the number."

Asher didn't back down. He never did. Raising his chin, he held her golden brown eyes with his dark blue ones. "Although you have seen fit to choose quite a menagerie of partners in the past, it was my understanding you had *invited* them to share your favors." His gaze flickered downward. "Unlike this mongrel."

Sophia felt her face flush. "Don't call him that."

Sam, still kneeling at Zach's side, said, "Asher doesn't have the strength to admit Zachary was a victim of his own brother's—and my—recklessness."

"On the contrary," Asher said. "I'm quite able to admit you and Gavin were unforgivably reckless to allow the existence of a creature who threatens not only the physical and mental health of my beloved sister but the continued safety of my kind's way of life."

"Give me a break," Sophia said, kneeling in solidarity next to Sam and Zach. "You're exaggerating." She wanted to touch Zach but stopped herself when an unfamiliar shyness gripped her.

Asher's voice struck like the needle-sharp dart that had felled Zach. "I exaggerate nothing. The danger of him shifting in the Platinum Club, which at this moment contains the governor of a major state, a former FBI director, and a pair of gate-crashing journalists from television, not to mention the other humans now walking around with video devices on their phones, cannot be understated. You don't think the sight of a werewolf would threaten our privacy and independence?"

"They didn't see him," Sophia said.

"Only because you removed him just in time," Asher replied. He pushed Zach's motionless leg with the toe of a custom-made leather shoe. "You're unlikely to be there on the next inevitable occasion."

Sam slapped Asher's foot away. "Don't you kick him. He's suffered enough. Do you realize it took two months before the poor man could even walk without assistance?"

"I'm quite aware of the extent of the damage done to him," Asher said. "Which is why I insist he be removed immediately to the clinic, where he and everyone else will be safe. The only alternative is elimination."

Sophia felt as if she'd been smacked in the stomach with a cannonball. Her lungs emptied of air, her eyes burned, and her heart squeezed painfully inward. She slumped forward, resting her hands over Zach's broad chest for support.

And immediately regretted it. The contact only amplified the emotions churning through her. She jerked her hands away, blinking back tears and fighting for breath.

What the hell was the matter with her?

While Sophia was falling apart on the floor, Sam jumped to

her feet to deal with Asher.

"What did you say?" Sam demanded. "Elimination?"

"You heard me," Asher replied. "If it had been up to me, that step would've been taken immediately, preventing today's situation from arising."

"You don't mean that," Sam whispered.

"Surely I do. It would also have prevented the months of indescribable suffering I understand he endured. In the recent past, even a full-breed born shifter could die if he failed to make his first shift until after he'd reached full maturity. The adult body simply isn't designed for such changes. An adult human . . . Well, it was cruel to keep him alive."

Sam's skin was almost as bright as her stunning red hair, and her eyes were wide and sparking with outrage. "You . . . you . . . you can't . . . ." Her voice caught in her throat.

Sophia, recovering from her second shock of the day, rose to her feet and put herself between Asher and the kind doctor. At his core, Asher's problem was not caring too little but too much. Her big brother could be an insufferable pain in the arse and an arrogant bully of the first order, but Sophia knew a horrible tragedy was to blame for the man he was today. She would never forget what he was like when she was little, how he taught her how to read, how to swim, laughing and playing with her when nobody else would take the time. How she'd idolized and adored him, the most handsome and charming of her (too many) brothers.

And then his wife, Claire, and their baby had died. And with them, a major portion of Asher's heart.

Those days were long, long ago, but Sophia held them in her heart, praying silently for a future in which the memories wouldn't seem like a strange, impossible dream.

"Where is the clinic?" Sophia asked. "I'll see to it he's taken there." She wouldn't risk touching him again, but she'd call for Derry. He could lift two werewolves and a fellow bear shifter without breaking a sweat.

"No!" Sam got between Sophia and Asher. "You can't send him back there. He was there long enough."

"Obviously not," Asher replied.

"He can't be held a prisoner any longer," Sam said. "He's strong and healthy, fully recovered—"

"Too strong," Asher said. "Too healthy." He gave Sophia a dark glance.

Suddenly remembering all those strong, healthy parts that had embraced her and promised to take her completely, Sophia's heart began to race. If Zach were experiencing the involuntary shifts and sexual aggression of shifter adolescence, he couldn't be wandering around the streets of Boston. A sexually sophisticated bear shifter like Sophia wasn't in any danger, but every other woman could be.

Because if he touched another woman, Sophia would kill her.

Wait. What? No! She'd kill *him*. *Him*.

Except she wouldn't kill him. That would be wrong. Like Sam said, he was the victim here. She had to think of Zach as a pitiable, inexperienced being, or else she'd be obligated to teach him a lesson.

A firm, deliciously slow lesson.

No, no, no.

"I agree with Asher," Sophia blurted. "He has to go back to the clinic."

"He can't," Sam said, her voice rising. "He just can't. It's not designed for long-term accommodation. Heck, it's not designed for short-term accommodation. It's just a makeshift space where we could keep an eye on him and shifter-specialist physicians could keep him alive. There's a treadmill and a TV and a tiny patio where he can look at the sky, but it's no way to live. He won't stay. We don't have the power to stop him. That's why he has patio access, actually. He broke a door and followed me out there a few weeks ago, and I didn't have the heart to refuse."

Asher, who had leaned over to inspect a scar on Zach's shoulder, suddenly turned and spun to face Sam. "Did he touch you?"

His low voice sent a shiver down Sophia's spine.

"Of course not!" Sam snapped. "He just wanted some fresh air."

"I'll increase security. I'll hire the best in the business," Asher said. "You—Everyone will be safe."

Sam's complexion turned a darker shade of red. "I—we—are completely safe from Zachary, I promise you."

"You don't know that. You don't know shifters. You have no idea what we're capable of. What damage we can do to human beings." Asher's voice dropped so low it was almost inaudible. "We can destroy you."

Sophia forced herself to look honestly at Zach—scarred, traumatized, unconscious—and see the truth in what Asher was saying. The man had nearly died and had a broken life ahead of him that they, the Stanton family if not all shifters, were responsible for.

When she had gone to nursing school, even her own family couldn't understand why the fun-loving, daring, independent—and filthy rich—Sophia Stanton had done it. But she had an impulse to care for people that she kept carefully hidden, even from her twin, Derry. It was an impulse that could get her into trouble, and she always regretted indulging in it.

Like now.

"We can't send him back to the clinic," Sophia said.

"Oh thank you, Sophia," Sam said. "Thank you for under-standing. He never would've harmed you, of course. In all these months, not once has he touched another human being. Or shifter. Not once."

Sophia was annoyed at how smug she was to hear that.

"It's not up to my sister to decide," Asher said. "He's too dangerous."

"He is," Sophia agreed. "I'm sorry, Sam, but you might not realize the harm he could do."

"Precisely," Asher said. "Your logic is slow to develop, Sophia, but I'm glad it won out in the end. I'll call Morgan to have him brought to the clinic, and then we can—"

"No, Asher," Sophia said. "There's another option."

Sam's hands flew up to her mouth. "No! Surely you don't mean . . ."

Sophia shuddered at the thought of harm coming to this man. *No, he was a novice, a changeling. Don't forget he's little more than a pitiable adolescent.*

And he's mine.

"Of course not," Sophia said, pulling out her phone to sum-mon the pilot of the Stanton's private jet. "He'll have to go to the ranch."

"Ranch?" Sam asked. "Do you mean . . ."

"Yep. Montana." Sophia texted Roger the time he should ex-pect them. "He won't be able to do any real harm way out there. That's why we have the place."

Asher began to protest but then seemed to see something in Sam's face. She looked so hopeful, so grateful—and, Sophia thought with amusement, more than a little beautiful. Asher was arrogant and impossible, but he was still a man.

"All right," he said carefully, eyes narrowed in skepticism. "But remember, Sophia. It was your idea."

Books by Diana Seere

THE BILLIONAIRE SHIFTERS CLUB SERIES

The Billionaire Shifter's Curvy Match

The Billionaire Shifter's Virgin Mate

The Billionaire Shifter's Second Chance

The Billionaire Shifter's Secret Baby

The Billionaire Shifter's True Alpha

Howls Romance

Classic romance . . . with a furry twist!
Did you enjoy this Howls Romance story?
If YES, check out the other books in the Howls Romance line!

The Werewolf Tycoon's Baby by Celia Kyle

Pregnant with the Werelion King's Cub by Claire Pike

The Alpha's Secret Family by Jessie Lane

Royal Dragon's Baby by Anya Nowlan

The Werebear's Unwanted Bride by Marina Maddix

Hunted by the Dragon Duke by Mina Carter

The Billionaire Werewolf's Witch by Celia Kyle

Nine Months to a Werewolf Mating by Claire Pike

Blackmailed Into Having the Werewolf King's Baby by Milly Taiden

The Jaguar Tycoon by Bianca D'Arc

The Billionaire Werewolf Claims a Bride by K. Collins

Her Unbearable Protector by Reina Torres

The Alpha's Enemy Mate by Jessie Lane

About the Author

Diana Seere was raised by wolves in the forests outside Boston and San Francisco. The only time she spends in packs these days is at romance writing conventions. In truth, Diana is two New York Times and USA Today bestselling authors who decided to write shifter romance and have more fun. You can find "her" on Facebook at Diana Seere's Facebook Page: *http://www.facebook.com/dianaseere*

Sign up for her New Releases and Sales email newsletter here: eepurl.com/beUZnr

Made in the USA
San Bernardino, CA
20 May 2019